THE DOCTOR'S UNEXPECTED FAMILY

PORT PROVIDENT: HURRICANE HOPE
BOOK TWO

KRISTEN ETHRIDGE

LAUREL LOCK PUBLISHING

CONTENTS

A GIFT FOR YOU

Dear Reader,

Hope has come. And even though her winds and rain have gone, she's left an indelible imprint on Port Provident.

Hope does that in our own lives, too. When we have hope, we have everything. Hope is the persistent belief that where we are going is better than where we've been. It's the force that wakes us up in the morning, puts one foot in front of the other, and turns dreams into reality.

And in Port Provident, it turns storms into happily-ever-afters. I can't wait for you start The Doctor's Unexpected Family so you can meet Pete and Angela—and one special little girl named Celina. Pete has always had a vision to go abroad in the world and make his mark. A hometown girl at heart, Angela wants nothing more than to help Port Provident recover from Hurricane Hope. She knows that in any other town, the fury of the storm could have been a knockout blow.

But Port Provident is special. It's a town of not just Hurricane Hope, but hope, heart, and happily-ever-after. It's a place where everyday faith mixes with history and a diverse group of friends, family, and community members to create a place that brings out the best in all of us—even those of us reading these stories.

Nothing makes me happier than getting a note from a reader that says they love these stories. Hearing that the characters and the town and the themes brought to life in the Port Provident books makes everything about being a writer worthwhile.

Port Provident isn't just a place, it's a place to belong. It's a community that you can be a part of every time you pick up one of these books. I think readers want more stories that are uplifting and make us think of the good in the world—because regardless of what the news tells us, it's out there. And that's why I created Port Provident —a town for all of us to visit for a sweet escape.

I'd like to invite you to become a part of the Port Provident reader community today. Just go to www.kristenethridge.com. You'll see the box to join right at the top of the page.

I'll send you Layla and Ridge's story, *A Place to Find Love*. Layla's spent her whole life searching for a greater meaning in her life. She comes to Port Provident running on fumes, but once she meets Ridge, she begins a journey that fills her with more than she ever hoped for—faith, family, and a place to find the love she's always longed for.

Welcome to a Texas beachside town you can escape to anytime. I promise these stories will lift you up and leave you with a smile.

All the best,
Kristen

P.S... One of the best ways to get to know Port Provident even better is to get your *Passport to Port Provident*. It's a behind-the-scenes reader exclusive that's available when you join me on Facebook Messenger at www.facebook.com/kristenethridgebooks

www.kristenethridge.com
www.facebook.com/kristenethridgebooks
www.instagram.com/kristenethridge

"*I* heard someone needs a doctor here?" Dr. Pete Shipley stopped the first person he saw. He'd received an urgent call about five minutes ago and had grabbed his things and come as fast as he could. The caller said only that Gloria needed him to come help. They'd quickly hung up before Pete had a chance to ask any questions.

He had no idea what he was walking into.

"Oh, back there in the corner by the parking lot. There's a pretty big crowd. You can't miss it." The teenage boy pointed to the left, off in the distance.

Pete hesitated. He wasn't quite sure how he'd get anywhere near where he was needed. There didn't seem to be any kind of clear path. Scratch that. There didn't seem to be any kind of path at all. He'd heard about the tent city that had popped up behind the elementary school in the middle of Port Provident as people began to return from evacuations necessitated by Hurricane Hope's recent landfall. Many of them crossed the causeway with anticipation, only to find that their homes were no longer suitable to live in and there was nowhere to go.

Most of the hotels in Port Provident had at least some level of damage, which drastically limited the number of available rooms. What rooms there were had been taken over by officials, disaster recovery specialists, and contractors. You had to know someone to get a hotel room in Port Provident in the wake of Hurricane Hope—and you had to have a bank account that could handle the cost because all the insurance and federal disaster hotel coverage hadn't fully kicked in yet. Most of the people in the lowest-lying neighborhoods, like the working-class *La Missión* neighborhood, didn't have any of those options.

And so, hundreds of tents and trailers and tarps had come together to form a makeshift community on the edge of the Texas coast. Pete surveyed the scene in front of him, certain he'd seen something like this before.

He had. Last summer on a medical mission trip to a refugee camp in the middle of Africa, hard hit first by the brutality of their fellow man and then further kicked by a deadly virus that thrived in the heat and the lack of hygiene and proper nutrition, he'd seen a refugee camp and the experience would stay with him forever.

Pete closed his eyes for a brief moment, took a deep breath into his lungs, and said a short prayer that the conditions which exacerbated the situation he'd seen in central Africa would not silently stalk in at this refugee camp in his own backyard.

He made his way to the group of people clustered around a beach chair set up in front of a boxy, green two-room tent.

"Gloria," he said, spotting the nurse-midwife who'd been a colleague of his before the wind and waves of Hurricane Hope had destroyed the Provident Women's Health and Birth Center where he'd served as Medical Director. "What's going on?"

"It's Angela Ruiz, the city councilwoman. Do you know her?" Gloria held the woman's hand as she sat, half-slumped in the chair.

Pete shook his head, then pulled his stethoscope out of a blue nylon bag.

"She was talking with some men who had brought a big utility-type truck full of items donated from by a church outside of Dallas, and then she just slumped to the ground. We got Angela moved here to the chair, and someone sent a truck over to see Angela's nephew, the pastor *at La Iglesia de la Luz del Mundo*. I'm just glad I was here bringing food that my parents cooked for some of their friends who are staying here."

Pete checked Angela's vitals and started trying to put two-and-two together. As he took a visual inventory of bodily signs like pupil dilation and rate of respiration, a few other things caught his eye. She had long, brown hair that had been swept back in a messy ponytail. Like everyone else nearby, a sheen of perspiration was clearly visible at the edge of her hairline. Her skin was an olive tone, and there was a hint on her cheeks of too much time spent in the recent sun.

"Please help my mama. She's di-betic." A little girl with raven-black, stick-straight pigtails hovered so close to the chair that she could have been fastened there with adhesive.

"This is your mom?" Pete squatted down low, trying to meet the little girl's eyes as he spoke. He flattened two fingers against the side of the woman's wrist and tried to keep track of her pulse. "I'm going to take care of her."

If the woman was diabetic, that pretty much took all the guesswork out of trying to diagnose her. "Type one or type two?"

She lifted one finger about halfway. It trembled a little bit and her whole arm slouched under the weight of a small, simple exertion.

"Angela, listen to me. Where's your Glucagon? Where's your monitor? Do you have any glucose tablets in your purse or anything?" He tried to keep his voice steady. He didn't want to upset the little girl any more than she already was. But at the same time, he had a sinking feeling about how successful Angela Ruiz could be at managing insulin-dependent diabetes in a place that could best be described as a tent city.

She feebly shook her head and tried to answer as best she could. "No tablets. I don't have any Glucagon here. My levels are all off because my monitor got wet during the storm and I don't think it's reading right, and I'm almost out of insulin, anyway. What I do have is at my office. I go there and take it these days."

"So you don't have any insulin here? And you're almost out? What type of insulin are you taking? What's the dosage?"

She shook her head subtly, then gave the details of her prescription.

He kept two fingers on her pulse and then shouted to be heard over the gathering crowd. "I need juice or even a soda or something. Right now. Gloria, I think I have a glucose monitor in my blue bag. Can you grab it for me? I need to know exactly what we're dealing with here. And can someone bring a soda over here?"

Pete was almost positive he was going to get a confirmation of hypoglycemia. And considering all the conditions in front of him, the only fairly effective treatment he had even a remote chance of finding in a cluster of refugee tents was a can of soda. If someone could find him one now, he could start helping her raise her sugar levels as soon as he had the monitor's results back.

Gloria pulled the gray plastic monitor from the bag, and another bystander ran to an ice chest, a few tents away. "If the clinic had been open, I'd have been comfortable handling this myself. But my monitor was not in the box of supplies I brought with me during the storm, so it's ruined. Pretty much like most of the tools of my trade. I'm glad you have one in your bag."

Pete found the equipment he was looking for in his bag. He pricked her finger quickly and stuck the test strip in the machine. He waited for the beep and then saw exactly what he knew he'd see. Thankfully, a lady handed him a red can of soda just at that moment.

"Yep, your blood glucose level is right at 70. That's very low." He popped the can of soda open and handed it to her. "Drink up, a little less than half that can. Then we'll give you about fifteen minutes and test you again."

The little girl reached for her mother's hand and tugged. "You okay, Mama?"

"Come here, *mija*." The councilwoman adjusted her position in the small chair and motioned for her daughter to climb in his lap.

Pete thought that was a bad idea—her balance was likely to be affected from the low blood sugar, and another body in that wobbly chair would likely be the precursor to a tumble on the ground for both of them. And then he'd have another medical issue on his hands. He started to say something, then stopped.

The fear slipped from the little girl's eyes as she snuggled her head

4

under her mother's chin. A few strokes across the crown of her head, and she'd completely relaxed. There was no medicine like a mother's love.

Gloria tugged at Pete's sleeve. "Hey, I can sit here with Angela for a few minutes, if you don't mind going to that tent over there and checking on Marisa Sanchez. I'm pretty sure it's dehydration, but again, I don't have so much as a stethoscope with me. Do you think you could just give her a look and see what you think she should do?"

Pete thought of the trash bags at the clinic waiting to be hauled out to the curb. They weren't really going anywhere—just the makeshift debris collection area at the back of the abandoned waterpark toward the middle of the island that he'd nicknamed "Mt. Dumpster." He didn't really have anything to go back for. And once he was finished with the lonely task of taking to the curb the last the trash that had been the heart and soul of the birth center his aunt and uncle founded fifteen years ago, then Pete would go home—a place that was just as lonely. He'd been in Port Provident for almost five years now, and still had nearly as few connections to the place today as he did the first time he drove over the causeway linking Provident Island to the Texas mainland.

"Sure, Gloria. I can go take a look. Where is she?"

Gloria pointed to a dark green tent, covered by a black tarp. "That's her husband standing out front. Just tell him who you are and that I sent you over."

It was no surprise to him that Gloria seemingly knew everyone. As isolated as he sometimes felt in Port Provident, Gloria was connected. She'd grown up in Port Provident, her parents owned a popular local restaurant near the beach, and her sister, Gracie, had married a member of the island's oldest and best-known families a few years ago. Even in the midst of all the craziness that Hurricane Hope had rained down on Port Provident, Gloria had reconnected with her high school sweetheart on the night the storm made landfall and was now in the first weeks of a re-blooming relationship.

If he was honest, Pete envied that. His high school sweetheart wasn't coming back into his life, at least not on this side of Heaven.

When Anna—who later became his fiancée—lost her battle with cancer, Pete had made some changes in his life.

One was coming to Port Provident to take over the clinic for his aunt and uncle.

The other was to put all the dreams he'd had for the future aside. He'd once thought he was that white-picket-fence-and-two-point-five-kids kind of guy. But without Anna, reminders of that dream were more like nightmares. And in a town like Port Provident, with block after block of historic Victorian homes, there were a lot of picket fences—and the ache that came with seeing them hadn't faded with time, as Pete had hoped.

It was time to move on. He was closing the clinic for good and had already applied to join the Mercy Medical Mission team full-time. He wanted to go to a place where he could both remove himself from reminders of Anna and finally use his medical skills to help heal people who had no access to the quality of care he was used to as a doctor in the western medical system.

He was so close to a new beginning. But since he still had at least a few weeks in Port Provident, he had time to do Gloria and her friends a favor.

"How is she?" Pete stopped in front of a skinny young man in his early twenties. "I'm Dr. Pete Shipley. Gloria Rodriguez sent me over."

"She's doing ok, I think. She gets a little dizzy when she sits up. She tells me she's fine, but I can see it in her eyes."

The young man shot a quick glance into the tent. Pete followed the direction of the young man's eyes and saw an equally young woman lying on an air mattress with pillows propped all around her. She was also clearly in an advanced state of pregnancy. He ducked through the cut-out that served as the door to the tent, then motioned at Pete to follow him.

"Marisa, this is Dr. Pete Shipley. Gloria asked him to come check you out. He's going to make sure you're ok."

Pete put his hand out to shake, but the girl only gave a stubborn glance at him, then focused her eyes back on Angela and the young man who'd squeezed into the fabric dome behind them.

6

"I'm fine. Quit making a big fuss over me."

There was no mistaking the tone in her voice. But her breathing also looked a little shallow, and Pete felt like her bravado was covering up a maternal fear that something was indeed very, very wrong.

"Marisa, could I just ask you a few questions? You're right, this is probably nothing, but I'd really like to make sure of that—and I'm sure your friends and family would too. It won't take but a few minutes." Pete dropped down and squatted at the corner of the air mattress as he spoke, in an attempt to get at eye level with his recalcitrant patient.

Her lips pressed together so hard that they began to blanch. They also looked dry and scaly. The skin under her eyes was sunken and gray as well. Pete started adding the signs together, putting his observations on a mental checklist.

"Can we just talk for a second?" Pete tried again after he got no response. Before he'd taken over the birth center for his aunt and uncle, Pete had spent several years as an emergency room physician, where he'd encountered just about every personality type under the sun.

Stubborn women were practically a specialty of his.

Marisa bit her lip, then nodded briefly. "But *he* needs to leave."

The tilt of her head left no doubt as to who she meant.

"Ok, Marisa, I'll just stand right outside." Her husband turned pointed outside, then ducked back through the tent's door.

Alone with his patient, Pete decided not to waste any more time on pleasantries. He didn't know when Marisa would declare the interview over. She clearly was not in a mood to chat or be fussed over.

"How much have you had to drink today?"

Pete opened the blue bag he'd placed on the floor in front of him and rummaged for his stethoscope, then he put it on and placed the flat disc over Marisa's heart as he waited for her answer.

"I don't know. Some orange juice this morning and a soda at lunch."

"And that's it? No water? Nothing else?" Her heart rate was a little fast, but nothing far out of the ordinary.

The young mother-to-be shook her head.

7

Pete put the stethoscope back and pulled out a small white box, a portable fetal Doppler, and a tube of gel.

"This'll be cold, so brace yourself." He squirted a little dollop of blue goop on her rounded abdomen, then began to slide the Doppler's little ultrasound attachment around. "Ok, and what have you had to eat?"

She closed her eyes as the *whoosh-whoosh* of the baby's heartbeat came through the small plastic speaker. "One of those little boxes of fruit-flavored cereal this morning, and some peanut butter crackers and a bag of sour cream and onion chips at lunch."

Pete didn't like what he was hearing. "That's all you've had to eat and drink all day?"

"It's all we've got. They don't have room service here."

Pete raised his eyebrows. She had him there. This parking lot was a disorganized mess. He clicked off the Doppler, then pulled out a towel and wiped the gel off both Marisa and his little machine before stowing everything back in the bag.

"Can you put out your arm?"

Marisa did as she was asked. Pete placed her hand atop one of his. Then with his other hand, he gave the skin on the back of her hand a pinch, holding it for a second before releasing. As he suspected, it stayed peaked like a little tent for longer than it should have. Decreased skin turgor was a classic sign of dehydration.

And dehydration was a gateway to a variety of adverse outcomes in a pregnant woman, including fainting spells.

Pete rocked back on his heels, still squatting nearby, but trying to give her a little space. "So, Marisa, tell me how things have been for you since the storm."

Marisa's eyelids popped open, then she rolled her eyes and made an indelicate grunt in reply.

"I know, dumb question, right?"

She made another grunt, then fell silent for a moment before answering. "The worst."

"How'd you come to be here at the tent city?" Pete decided to keep gently holding the hand he'd done the pinch test on. Sometimes, patients just needed to know someone was there for them, looking out for them.

"We lived in Coronado Heights," she said, naming one of the city's subsidized housing developments on the edge of the *La Missión* area of town. "Our place was on the first floor. They told us that the water was up to the ceiling. Everything's gone. They won't even let us go back inside. It's just all gone. "

Marisa took an uneven breath, then looked up at the top of the tent with an intense gaze. "My husband lost his job after Labor Day weekend. The tourist season was over, and they'd had a slow year. So now we don't have any insurance. The hospital's closed, but I couldn't afford a doctor bill anyway right now. No job, no home, no money. No nothing. What kind of mother am I, bringing a child into all this mess?"

A sob shook her chest as the tears started to flow. Pete could see the burden of her circumstances pressing down on her, suffocating her dreams and tearing apart her security net.

"I understand." Pete gave her hand a gentle squeeze and hoped he sounded reassuring.

"How? How could you possibly understand, Mr. Fancy Doctor?" She pulled her gaze from the top of the tent and turned her head to look at Pete. A hint of sheepishness crossed her face. "Sorry. That wasn't very nice."

A lump of ice hit Pete square in the throat. He'd hoped to be compassionate. He wanted to explain what he meant, but knew no matter what he said, it wouldn't be adequate.

"Well, I lost my job too. The clinic where I work was destroyed by the hurricane, and we won't be re-opening."

"Oh," Marisa said flatly. "But you're a doctor. You can get another job, right?"

Pete thought of his application for Mercy Medical Mission, taken with a friend to Houston two days ago so it could be mailed, as mail service on Provident Island had been suspended since Hope. His uncle knew the medical director of the organization and had already made a few phone calls, so the actual application was more or less a formality, pending an opening coming available. "I hope so. I don't really know where I'll be or what I'll be doing, though. I do know something I can do right now, though."

Marisa pulled her hand back, then tried to lift herself into a half-sitting position on her elbows. "What?"

"I know the head of obstetrics over at Mainland Medical, the next closest hospital to us. It had very minor hurricane damage, so it's open and accepting patients. I'll call my friend and arrange to get you checked out, free of charge, and get you back with routine prenatal care. I think you're pretty severely dehydrated and I believe you have a condition called vasovagal syncope."

Her brown eyes widened. "That sounds serious."

"It's when the part of your nervous system that regulates heart rate and blood pressure malfunctions in response to a trigger. Your heart rate slows, and the blood vessels in your legs widen. This allows blood to pool in your legs, which lowers your blood pressure. This drop in blood pressure and slowed heart rate quickly diminish blood flow to your brain, and you faint." Pete had seen this happen many times over the years, and was as certain as he could be without labs and other diagnostic tests. "It can be triggered by things like stress and dehydration, and you've got plenty of both. I want you to spend a couple of days in the hospital, getting IV fluids and regular meals and getting you and the baby checked out to make sure that there are no other underlying causes. Dr. Mitchell will make sure you get the best possible care."

"You promise they're not going to care that I can't pay?" She seemed so scared, so unsure.

Pete nodded. "I promise. I'm going to talk to Dr. Mitchell personally. In fact, I'm going to step outside and make the call. Do you want me to send your husband back in?"

Marisa rubbed her belly and nodded. "Ok. Thank you, Dr. Shipley."

"You're welcome." Pete smiled. He hadn't done much, but if he'd eased even a fraction of her stress and worry, he'd consider today a success.

He motioned to Marisa's husband, pacing just a few steps away. "I'm pretty sure they'll both be fine. I want her to go to Mainland Medical to get checked out and to get some fluids for her dehydration."

"We can't—"

Pete cut off Marisa's husband before he could start. There was no need for the man to air their situation out in front of the gathered crowd. "I know. I've already told Marisa I'll take care of everything."

"Everything?" The young man looked at Pete with hope and gratitude.

"Everything." And he meant it, even if Pete couldn't work out a *pro bono* arrangement and had to tell Dan Mitchell to send the bill straight to him.

Marisa's husband disappeared inside the tent. Pete reached in his pocket for his cell phone, but decided to check in with Angela before he made the phone call, in case he needed to find two beds at Mainland instead of just the one for Marisa.

"She's going to be okay?"

Angela's arms were crossed over her chest tightly. Pete couldn't tell if she was trying to keep something in or something out.

"I think it's stress and dehydration. I picked up good fetal heart tones on my portable Doppler, so I think the baby's fine. A few days at Mainland Medical getting real food and some IV fluids should have Marisa good as new. I'm going to make the arrangements, but in the meantime, I need to get Gloria to go over to the Samaritan's Cross medical trailer and get me a bottle of a sports beverage with electrolytes. They should have some on hand. Where is Gloria? I thought she was staying here with you."

"She was, but the Bordegos needed her to look at their daughter. She's got an upset stomach, and they're concerned. No one wants a stomach bug to break out in here." Angela nodded her head in the direction of a tent a few feet away. "And the Samaritan's Cross relief team is delayed. They won't be here for another two to three days."

That didn't sound right to Pete. "Aren't they always the first on the scene of every disaster?"

"Well, before Hurricane Hope, the local Samaritan's Cross team had arrangements with 10 different locations in town for shelters and command centers. But then the storm surge blew the doors off of every prediction and every single place the Samaritan's Cross team had identified—including their main office downtown—was flooded and not able to be used. So they're scrambling, and we're just using what supplies are being trucked in from over the causeway on a day-to-day basis."

That threw a wrench into Pete's plans. He wanted to start treating Marisa's dehydration as soon as possible. He looked around the sea of people and felt even more hopeless about the situation surrounding him. Not only had most of these people suffered catastrophic losses, like Marisa, and were forced to live in this crazy situation temporarily, but even the groups who should have been providing basic relief weren't here.

These folks literally had nothing right now.

"I see Gloria. Looks like she's walking back this way. Let me see if she has any ideas."

Pete met Gloria about halfway and quickly gave her an overview of the situation. They discussed a few options, then she decided she would use her connections with the Port Provident Beach Patrol to bring a few bottles of sports drink and some peanut butter crackers—or anything with protein—over to the tent city from the Beach Patrol's official stash of supplies.

It was a bit like putting together a puzzle. Not your typical medicine. He liked it, and he couldn't wait until everything was straightened out with Mercy Medical Mission and he was doing this kind of work full-time.

As he waited for Gloria, he called Dan Mitchell, who was more than happy to open his practice to Marisa and assured Pete that no compensation would be necessary. He agreed with Pete that Marisa had been through enough and needed a dose of compassion in addition to some medical care.

Gloria arrived back about fifteen minutes later, a loaded plastic bag in one hand. "What'cha thinking, boss?"

"I'm not your boss anymore."

She smiled broadly. "*Sí.* What'cha thinking, Doctor-Who-Used-to-Be-My-Boss?"

Pete laughed a little at her new salutation. It was good to see this transformation in Gloria, who'd once been serious enough for everyone on staff in the clinic. Losing her home and her job to the hurricane—and reconnecting with her former boyfriend, Chief Rigo Vasquez of the Port Provident Beach Patrol—had seemed to free Gloria in a way. She'd been able to let the wind and the waves drive away her past and embrace the future to come.

It fascinated Pete.

In fact, it inspired Pete. Maybe there would be a new beginning like that for him soon. "I was thinking about puzzle pieces."

"Gloria!" Angela raised her voice a bit and waved her hand. "Did you get those for Marisa?"

Gloria nodded and waved a bottle of blue liquid. "Yes, I was able to get some sports drinks from Rigo's stash at the temporary Beach Patrol headquarters. Rigo will actually be here in a few minutes, and we'll take her to Mainland Medical, if you've got everything set up, Pete."

"Just got off the phone with Dan Mitchell. Everything's set. Great thinking on having Rigo take her there—I assume he's got emergency medical training because of his work on Beach Patrol, right?"

Gloria nodded. "Absolutely. An extra level of precaution, just in case. We could even flip the lights on the truck on if we needed to."

"I'm pretty sure you won't need to, Gloria. She's pretty stable. Just needs a saline IV, some real food and some TLC." Pete took the bag and bottle from Gloria's hands and turned back toward Marisa's tent.

Within minutes, Rigo drove his truck over the narrow strip of grass at the fenceline and parked nearby.

"Pete," Gloria called, "Rigo's here. It's time to get Marisa in the truck."

Marisa shuffled out, Pete supporting her under one arm and Rodgie, her husband, holding up the other side. A duffel bag was slung over Rodgie's shoulder, and a deep poke of pain hit Pete's heart as he realized that duffle bag likely held all of their few remaining possessions.

Gloria darted over to the passenger side door and opened it before Marisa got there, then everyone took care to get the young mother-to-be in the truck and make her comfortable. Pete watched Rodgie tuck the duffel bag on the floorboard at Marisa's feet and felt that sting of sharp metal in his chest again.

Please keep them safe and healthy, God, she thought silently. *Give them some rest and renew their spirit—just like we all need right now.*

Rodgie climbed in the back seat of the truck behind Rigo, and Gloria closed the passenger side door in the front seat, and just like that, they were off.

"Brought you something." About two hours later, Gloria stuck her head through the flap of Angela's tent. She held up a small cooler and wiggled it.

"I hope that has an iced coffee and a real dinner in it." Angela laid down the folder of papers she'd been reviewing.

It had been a few hours since this afternoon's drama, and as her blood sugar rose, Angela had decided to just sit on her sleeping bag and go over the data about temporary housing sites she'd been given that morning by FEMA. She couldn't decide if her headache was a lingering effect of the earlier insulin rollercoaster or because she was so frustrated that this program that her constituents desperately needed was so wrapped in red-tape.

Gloria shrugged. "Well, no, but I passed the Samaritan's Cross food truck when I turned on 51st Street. I guess they'll be here within the hour or so."

"I said a real dinner. I miss food. Real food. I just want to go to Porter's and have a shrimp po-boy or to *Huarache's* and eat my weight in those amazing pork tamales your *madre* makes. I should miss real things, like my daughter's baby book or my parents' wedding portrait that used to hang in my hallway. But no. Food. I think about a real meal morning, noon, and night."

Gloria ducked and came inside the tent. "Well, most people think about food morning, noon, and night. It's called breakfast, lunch, and dinner."

Angela's stomach gave a little gurgle. "Not quite what I meant. So, what's in the cooler if it's not something iced down and caffeinated?"

"Insulin." Gloria gave the blue and white rectangle a little shake. "There's a glucagon kit in there too."

Angela raised her brows. "Insulin? Did you go to City Hall and get my last vial or something?"

"Nope. Pete called the pharmacy at Mainland Medical and had me do a pick up for you while we were dropping Marisa off. This is Rigo's cooler. There's no ice in here because I didn't want it to freeze. I just didn't want it to get too hot. September on the Gulf Coast is brutal on everyone, especially something delicate like insulin."

Angela blew out a strong, deep breath. "Yeah, it is. Thank you, Gloria. I've been asking for a few days if there was a resource to get me more insulin. I've been skipping doses to stretch it. Of course, I've been skipping a few meals too, so I tried to tell myself it all balanced out."

"Angela, you've got to take care of yourself. Times are crazy right now, I know. But you can't sacrifice your health." Gloria sat down, cross-legged, on the end of Celina's sleeping bag. "Especially for Celina. She needs her mother, and she needs her to be well."

"I know, Gloria. I'm trying, really, I am. But it's like everyone has a question or a need or something right now. I've been hiding in here reading these FEMA briefs, and I think it's the longest stretch of alone-time I've gotten since Hope hit."

Gloria shifted slightly, opening her mouth, then closing it again without speaking.

"What?" Angela questioned.

"Do you think it would help if Celina went and stayed with her dad for a few weeks until the worst of this is over?"

Angela felt a lick of fire flare in her chest. "Absolutely not. Gloria, if you think I'm overworked and inattentive, you can't possibly think David is a good option. He is a workaholic. He doesn't even know Celina—by his own choice."

"I know he's not involved, Angela. I just know he's got a good job and I assume a good house and such now. I thought maybe getting Celina out of the elements and this crazy tent city might be better for her, just temporarily."

Angela picked up the FEMA paperwork and waved it. The pile made a satisfying slapping sound as she threw them back on the sleeping bag. "What will make things better for everyone is when the bureaucrats cut the red tape and get the trailers here so people have real shelter. Celina belongs with me, Gloria. Not someone who is biologically related to her, yet doesn't know anything about her."

She pushed a hand through her hair and tried not to let her frustration with her ex-husband get the best of her. He was not worth tanking her blood sugar over. The time for that had been six years ago. She had the well-being of thousands of constituents to worry about now, not one selfish man.

"You're probably right, Angie. I just hate seeing you here. I wish I had a bed to offer you, but I'm still crashing in the guest room at Inez Vasquez's house. My parents are crowded into a garage apartment with my sister, Gracie, and her husband and their baby. I just wish that our area of town hadn't been so badly hit so you could get out of here."

Angela cracked a wry smile. "There's no place I'd rather be than here, Gloria. I had the option to get a room at the Grand Provident. I gave it to Lola de la Vega. She needed it more than I did. She's been my assistant since my first campaign, and I owe her so much. I was glad to let her have my spot. This is a mess, but it's home. These are still my neighbors, still my constituents. And in a way, it's more important than ever that I'm here with them. I have a little fireside chat every night and tell them what happened today at City Hall. People don't have good access to TV or radio or phones or internet like they're used to. I keep them informed, and they tell me what they need. I can't leave them."

"So when do you think FEMA will bring the trailers?"

"I hope soon. They've backed out of two locations because of elevation concerns. This proposal is to clear out the old municipal baseball fields and put the trailer park in there. I don't really like that because it's so far from town, and there's no public transportation, obviously, so it'll be hard for people to get to grocery stores and work. Plus, we'll be starting from scratch, so it'll take a while to put in electricity and water and such. But it looks like the best option right now."

"And you'll go there?"

"That's my plan. We should have room for more than 150 trailers there. So that would be a good start." She tried to smile at her friend, but she was too tired to do more than barely tug the corners of her mouth upward. It had only been just over a week since the hurricane made landfall, but it felt like Angela had been sleeplessly living in a tent behind an elementary school her whole life. "Our community needs stability now, any kind we can get."

"The new normal, huh?" Gloria twisted her smile like a corkscrew. "Do you think you'll be okay here, Angela?"

Gloria gave the cooler a subtle push toward Angela.

"I've been diabetic practically my whole life, Glo. I was diagnosed when I was nine. I'll be fine."

Gloria pulled out her cell phone and tapped at the screen. "I just texted you Pete's contact information. Promise me you'll call him if you need anything? I'm going to be off the island tonight at a family dinner in Houston, and since the curfew will be on by the time I would get back, I'm just staying with my cousin Carla on the mainland."

Angela nodded. "Really, Gloria, I'll be fine. But I appreciate the concern. And thank you for bringing me a refill."

"Thank Pete. He took care of everything. I'm just the delivery lady." Gloria stood as much as she could, and then shuffled awkwardly to the door of the tent.

"And I appreciate it. Thanks for everything today, Gloria. I'm lucky to have a friend like you."

Gloria ducked out, then stuck her hand back through the curved fabric arch and waved her fingers in a gesture of goodbye.

Angela picked up her folder again and tried to focus on reading the documents on the temporary housing options FEMA was putting on the table. She could hear the sound of the Samaritan's Cross truck rumbling up. As soon as they were set up, they'd be swamped with a mass of hungry people from all over the tent community. The lines had been averaging almost two hours the last few nights.

As the person elected to represent the majority of the people now calling this patch of grass behind Provident Elementary School home, it made Angela's blood boil like a stock pot full of soup. She wanted her friends, her neighbors, her constituents to have their dignity and their lives back. The solutions presented in that manila folder weren't good enough.

There was so much that needed to be done in the wake of this huge, life-altering natural disaster. Knowing how long and winding and bumpy the road ahead would be, Angela paused and swallowed past the small lump forming in her throat.

Was *she* good enough to get it all done?

2

The late summer sun still stretched brightly in the streaked sky as Angela finished her dinner. Tonight's offering from the Samaritan's Cross mobile kitchen had been simple, but filling: a cheese sandwich with a surprisingly crisp leaf of lettuce and a cheerful wheel of bright red tomato, a cup of tomato soup, and an orange. Angela gave the orange a quick toss from hand to hand as she walked back to her tent.

Should Angela save the orange as a snack for Celina later, or should she eat it herself now as a sweet, juicy dessert?

Angela could almost taste the drips of fresh orange juice on her tongue. She looked at the gently dimpled peel of the orange and stopped herself before she dug in. Considering all of today's blood sugar drama, she should probably check her levels first. She'd headed to the food truck without taking her insulin shot first, and now that Gloria had replenished her supply, Angela mentally chastised herself. She knew what would happen if she didn't keep up with her regimen. Like many diabetics, she'd skipped a shot here or there and just stayed on top of her monitoring. But the batteries had run out of her monitor, and she hadn't been able to find anyone with extras—which led to the scare earlier today.

And goodness knows there wasn't a big box store or corner market open in Port Provident to get any replacement batteries.

Relying on a lifetime of instinct and observations when it came to insulin was not a recipe for success, and she knew it. Angela blew a heavy breath out of pursed lips. She was stuck. In a big way.

For the first time since Hurricane Hope rolled past, Angela was scared. She needed to keep her blood sugar in check. One missed shot wouldn't hurt her. Forty-eight hours without shots or monitoring could actually kill her. But what could she do?

Back in her tent, she sat down and pulled out her phone. Could she call the police and report a battery emergency? They probably got plenty of assault and battery calls, but probably not many three-volt lithium battery calls.

Seriously, Angela, she muttered to herself. *The police force is overwhelmed these days. You can't call them because you're out of batteries. If they have batteries to spare, they're probably double-As or nine-volts or something common like that. You can't be a pest.*

Absently, she scrolled on her phone. Then she saw the contact card Gloria had texted her earlier.

Well, obviously Pete Shipley had a working glucose monitor. And she had to admit that calling him made more sense than calling Port Provident PD.

She clicked on the phone number hyperlinked in the text.

"Pete Shipley."

Angela couldn't figure out why she was nervous to tell the doctor why she was calling. "Hi, Dr. Shipley, it's Angela Ruiz—Gloria's friend."

"Hi, Angela. You can call me Pete. Any friend of Gloria's is a friend of mine." His voice sounded as warm and soothing as the whipped milk on top of a designer cappuccino. "Is something wrong at the tent city? Did you get the insulin I asked Gloria to pick up?"

"No one else is sick. And I did get the insulin. Thank you very much. That's actually what I was calling about."

"Did I get the type wrong? I called in Humulin. Did you actually want Novolin?" He named off the two most popular brands of insulin.

"No, you got the right type. The problem is my monitor. It doesn't work, and I obviously can't take a shot without knowing what my numbers are. My battery is totally dead, and there's nowhere to get a lithium battery here right now. I won't be able to get to the mainland and back before the curfew goes into effect."

She hesitated before voicing her request, but she couldn't say exactly why.

"So you need to borrow my monitor?"

Pete completed Angela's sentence, and she relaxed a little bit.

"If I could, yes. I don't want to inconvenience you, but…"

Angela could hear shuffling noises in the background and a metallic sound that she suspected was the jingling of a set of keys. "Don't apologize, Angela. I should have left it with you earlier today. You can't give yourself a shot without knowing your glucose levels. That's dangerous. I was just finishing up some clean-out at the clinic, so I'll be there in about fifteen minutes. Can you wait that long?"

She didn't have any of the tell-tale signs of highly-fluctuating sugar. "I think that will be fine. Thank you, Pete."

"Not a problem, Angela. Happy to help a friend of Gloria's. I'll see you shortly."

He hung up the call, and Angela turned back to her paperwork. The longer she spent in this tent, the more resolved she became to know everything about the temporary housing issue. She needed to get her constituents back to safe housing so they could have stability in their lives.

Angela looked over at the little blue cooler in the corner, full of the insulin that was such a part of the routine of her own life.

Her constituents and neighbors weren't the only ones who needed some stability in their lives. She had read the reports, she sat in the meetings with officials and bureaucrats. She didn't have the luxury of *not* knowing just how steep the hill was for Port Provident to climb. She had a young daughter who missed her home and her favorite toys. And she herself had a health condition that needed to be managed. She couldn't afford to just blow off the necessary management of her condition, but living in a situation like her current one made the day-to-day difficult.

She had to get stability in her own life in order to bring stability to all the thousands of lives around her.

Angela frowned thoughtfully. She couldn't even manage an insulin shot right now. How could she help all the people who were depending on her?

For being an unemployed doctor in a town with no working medical facilities, Pete sure seemed to have a full patient load today. At least Pete felt confident that Marisa would be taken care of and back to full health in no time, thanks to the staff at Mainland Medical.

As far as Angela Ruiz was concerned, Pete wasn't quite as certain. She'd raised his doctor radar. He couldn't quite say what triggered it, but he knew to trust his instincts and keep asking questions until he figured out the puzzle.

He was glad she called. She'd been on his mind since he'd returned to the clinic. He wanted to tell himself it was all concern for her health, but the number of times he'd caught himself paused and thinking about her cocoa eyes instead of working on cleaning up the clinic was anything but healthy.

Pete wound through the maze of tents and set-ups that were more like lean-tos, and about a dozen other things in between. He found the tent that Angela had been sitting in front of earlier. He'd seen lots of insurance agents and government groups setting up temporary field offices in areas all over the city, and thought it was a good thing that Angela had set up a place here in this tent city so that the citizens of Port Provident had access to her—especially since everyone's access to radio, TV, and the Internet were very limited right now.

He gave a little knock on the tent to announce himself, and the fabric structure wobbled with the gentle taps.

"Come on in," said Angela's voice from the other side.

"How are you feeling? Any better?" Pete held up the glucose

monitor as he ducked through the opening. "Let's do a quick check so we can calibrate your insulin dosage."

Angela stuck out her pointer finger, and Pete swiped an alcohol wipe over it, then massaged the tip of her finger to get the blood flowing. He couldn't help but notice Angela's nails, the bright pink polish shredded and chipped on the ends. It struck him like a cosmetic metaphor for the woman next to him. She had fine, classic features, but he could tell she was frayed and worn out.

Quickly, he pricked the edge of her finger with the lancet, then fixed up a test strip and popped it in the monitor. He smiled a bit when he saw the reading.

"Rebounding nicely, just as I'd hoped." He showed Angela the digital display. A slow smile appeared across her face.

"Thanks, I'm sorry I made you come all the way back over here." She kept stroking the hair of the little girl sitting quietly in her lap. "I'll be fine. Thanks again for getting everything taken care of for Marisa at Mainland Medical Center. That was very generous of you."

"It was the right thing to do." Pete tucked all his supplies back in the blue bag. "And the right thing for *you* to do is get some rest and let your body get back to normal. I'd feel better if I saw you back to your house and got you settled before I go to my house for the evening."

"We can go home, Mama?" The little girl's eyes took on the look of donuts—perfectly round and sugar-glazed—as she lifted her head off Angela's shoulder. "I can see Huggy Lovey!"

Angela's own glance skimmed the top of her daughter's forehead, careful to not make eye contact before looking blankly out toward some trees in the distance. "Not today, sweetie, remember?"

The little girl shook her head, black pigtails flapping assertively.

"We have a lot of work to do before we can go home."

"Home probably wasn't the best choice of words. I can get you settled wherever you're staying, and then I can head back to what I was doing at the clinic."

"Really, Dr. Shipley, that's not necessary." Angela shifted her weight from her left hip to her right and twitched her shoulders.

"The name's Pete, remember? And it is necessary. You're my

patient now. And I take care of my patients. Especially now, when this corner of the world's a big mess." Pete stood up. "Now, where are you staying?"

Angela pursed her lips and the corner of her mouth twisted downward. She looked hesitant, a far cry from the stereotype that would be attached to someone in politics.

"There." The little girl pointed in the direction of the area behind Pete's foot.

He turned around furrowed his brow in concentration. He was beginning to put two and two together, and he didn't like how the equation was adding up.

"That's a sleeping bag. Is it yours?" Pete knelt down and got at eye level with the little face.

She nodded.

He'd been terribly wrong in his assumption when he walked up and knocked on the wall of the tent. "So, where is your house?"

"We live at 404 Houston Street. Huggy Lovey is still there, and I miss her." She spoke with the distinct syllables of childhood.

Houston Street. If he wasn't mistaken, that area, where streets were named for the heroes of the Texas Revolution, was one of the hardest-hit in all of Port Provident. That's where Gloria's house was. "You live in Alamo Court?"

"Lived." Angela jumped into the conversation with one charged syllable. Her voice sounded stronger, which Pete took as a good sign. "As Celina pointed out, we're staying here for right now."

Pete had a hard time believing his ears. "But you're a member of City Council. Surely there's someplace better for you to stay."

She fixed her gaze squarely on Pete's face. "This is where most of my constituents without homes are. They elected me to represent them. That doesn't make me better than them, or worthy of staying someplace special when they're stuck in a tent city because they don't have anywhere else to go and there's too much red tape keeping the people who are supposed to be helping from actually doing anything."

He could hear the conviction in her voice. It bordered on anger when she talked about the inefficiency of aid.

"I understand, and I didn't mean to say otherwise, Angela. But you're exhausted and not eating well, and you said it yourself—you aren't able to adequately keep up with your insulin levels. You can't help your people if you can't stay well."

"Things will be better in a few days. We'll make due until then."

"Angela, look around you. Look at your daughter. I know you've managed diabetes probably most of your life. You've got a routine. But when you're in a place where you can't manage that routine, it can become a life and death situation. You need to be somewhere that you can take care of your little girl and yourself."

Pete had no idea why his blood pressure was ticking up. He barely knew this woman. But his doctor's instinct had kicked in, and he wanted to fix this whole messed up situation. He couldn't fix everything on the island, but he *could* fix this.

"There isn't any place for me to go now, anyway. There aren't many hotels even open on the island to begin with. I was offered a room as a city councilmember, but I gave it to a lady on my staff. She needed it more than me." She picked up the soda can and lifted it to her lips for another drink.

Pete immediately knew what happened. She'd gotten a little defensive, and her fight-or-flight reflex had kicked in, the hormones and chemicals surging alongside the adrenaline messing up the delicate endocrinological balance Angela had just started to gain back.

"Your sugar's dropping again, isn't it?"

"You can't tell that just by looking at me."

"Actually, I can. You're starting to sweat just a little bit up along your hairline, and you're leaning back in your chair. Look, I don't know how to fix FEMA's issues, but I have more than a decade's worth of experience around medical patients. What's going to happen to your daughter when you pass out on that sleeping bag in the middle of the night, and there's no one to help you or take care of her? There's no 911 to call right now, no ambulances, and no hospital on the island to go to in the event of an emergency."

Angela looked up at Pete. Her brown eyes flashed with a small glint of lightning, then the feistiness dimmed and she turned her gaze down to her feet. "I don't know. But I truly don't know where to go now, either. Sure, there's actually power at my City Hall office, but there's no one else up there in the middle of the night if something were to happen to me. At least here, there's plenty of people we know."

"Plenty of people who don't know how to treat blood glucose reactions."

There was only one solution to this problem, crazy as it was. Pete decided not to beat around the bush, but instead to just come out and say it. Sometimes you needed to sugar coat things for your patients, but other times, you had to give it to them straight. This was definitely the latter.

"You just need to come back to my house. I have a guest room, and my home is on stilts, so it thankfully sustained almost no damage. This way, you're under a doctor's care. I can monitor your sugar and your diet, and you're not tied to the hours or offerings of the Samaritan's Cross truck, which I know are not exactly diabetic-friendly. Way too carb-heavy. What did you have for dinner tonight?"

Angela muttered something under her breath.

"I didn't hear you. But let me guess…white bread was involved, wasn't it?"

She looked up at him through her eyelashes. "Maybe."

"I've been practicing medicine long enough to know when a patient says 'maybe,' they actually mean yes. Especially when we're talking about bad diet choices."

"I don't have a choice! They serve what they serve. I'll be sure and have City Council request chefs from the Food Network to man the food trucks after the next hurricane."

"Angela, even Bobby Flay couldn't help you right now. You don't need a side of chipotle. You need a balanced meal with some protein and some low-glycemic offerings."

Pete couldn't keep from letting out a breath when he noticed Angela's nostrils flare slightly and her lips purse. He could see her protests crumbling in the face of the facts that she, as a life-long Type 1 diabetic, knew all too well.

"It's likely anyone would have struggled to maintain optimal blood sugar levels—even non-diabetics—in the stressful, uncertain environment created after Hurricane Hope rolled through Port Provident," Pete said. He didn't want her to talk herself out of what she knew deep inside. "But you're not just anyone. You're a Type 1 diabetic. You've been too lax with your numbers and your levels for too many days in a row now. You were very close to needing to go to the hospital today along with Marisa. This isn't just a matter of me telling you to watch your diet. You've got to get some help and stability because this is getting close to a life and death type of issue, and you know I'm right."

Angela nodded slowly. "Pete, I think maybe you're exaggerating just a little bit. I've had diabetes my whole life. It's not like I was just diagnosed last week and don't understand what I'm dealing with. Besides, I can't take my daughter to your house. I don't even know you."

"Well, to that point, I don't know you either. But we both know Gloria. I trust anyone who is a friend of hers, and I'd hope you'd feel the same."

"Of course I trust Gloria's judgment." Angela's voice was still. It reminded Pete of the calm of the eye in the middle of the hurricane not so long ago.

"So you'll come with me?"

Gloria shook her head, her brown hair softly dancing around her face. "Really, I'm fine. I've got the monitor. I've got the insulin. You don't need to worry about me."

Pete stuck his hand out and gave her the monitor. He didn't know her well, wasn't her physician of record, and didn't have any other way to convince her.

He said a brief goodbye to both Angela and Celina, then stooped to exit the tent, trying to convince himself that the nagging feeling in his midsection was just the remains of his own Samaritan's Cross food truck meal, and not the gut instinct honed from years on the front lines of medicine.

~

His bed was lumpy. After seeing how so many of his fellow citizens were sleeping, in tents and sleeping bags, Pete mentally chastised himself to ignore the fact that he couldn't get comfortable. But in spite of this, he kept shifting his position and mentally replaying the events from earlier in the day.

Angela had to be a practical woman. She'd been elected to the Port Provident City Council, and he remembered from the last election that she also helped run her family's small business. While he respected the fact that she'd been managing diabetes most of her life, he didn't understand why she seemed to agree with him, yet couldn't accept the help he was offering.

He rarely pushed aside his gut reaction. Part of being a good doctor was the balance of knowledge and instinct. Instinct pushed him to follow his knowledge down paths to solve his patients' health issues, or to proactively make decisions to keep them from ever having issues. Tonight, though, he made himself ignore that strong feeling.

He told the voice in his head to hush, rolled over again, and picked up the remote control to the TV. He'd come into his bedroom early, trying to wind down with a favorite movie recorded on his DVR, knowing he should enjoy the distraction while he could, since TV of any kind likely wouldn't be an option to unwind with wherever Mercy Medical Mission would probably send him. For now, though, he was still in the United States, where mindless TV would take his mind off everything that had happened lately.

Especially one epically stubborn, brown-eyed City Councilwoman.

The sound of his cell phone buzzing against the nightstand woke Pete up from a sound sleep. The blue light of the TV flickered from the corner, giving the whole room a strange glow. He must have fallen asleep while zoning out on reality TV.

"Dr. Shipley." The digital clock near the phone said it was too early to be asleep, but too late to be receiving social phone calls.

He didn't know what this call could possibly be about. All of his patients had been transferred to the care of doctors off the island since the clinic was now permanently closed and even Provident Medical

Center was shut down for the foreseeable future due to hurricane damage.

"Pete, it's Angela. I need your help."

Of all the calls this could have been, Angela asking for help didn't even make his top 100 list. She started talking so fast, his brain couldn't keep up.

"Whoa, whoa. What did you say?"

She paused, then thankfully spoke much more slowly. "There's been a shooting on the other side of the tent city. The police are here now."

"Angela, are you ok? Is Celina ok?" The brain fog induced by mindless television was completely gone now. Pete felt like a bolt of lightning had cracked under his bed, propelling him up into a sitting position.

"We're fine. It happened on the other side of the grounds. But the police are shutting this down. They're clearing everyone out right now and moving us to the high school. They're re-establishing a shelter there, like they had the shelter of last resort there the night of the hurricane."

He relaxed a little at the knowledge that Angela and her little pigtailed pixie of a daughter were okay. "So what do you need? Help taking down the tent and packing up?"

"My car is in the City Hall parking garage, and I need to get out of here. They've got the area on lockdown, but I think I can get the police to let you in. I told you I don't like using privileges that my constituents can't use. But this isn't for me. It's for my daughter." He could hear her take a deep breath and then he heard a small, muffled sob. "Celina is terrified of going to the shelter. She spent the night there during the hurricane with my sister Emmy, because I had to be working at the command center. She was terrified, and she doesn't want to go back. Can we still use your guest room?"

He knew there was a reason he couldn't dismiss that gut feeling earlier. He just didn't expect the reason to be something other than blood sugar.

But the truth was, he didn't blame Celina one bit. She'd been through enough in the very recent past to last her a lifetime. Whatever he could do to bring the smile back to her face, he would.

"I'm on my way."

"Thank you, Pete. Thank you for helping my daughter." She breathed a sigh of relief. "I wish I could fix things for everyone else here as easily."

3

There was too much to do right now for Angela to sit still, but her body was working against her. The adrenaline surge when she heard the distinctive "pop, pop" sound of gunfire and lunged to cover Celina with her own body made her feel lightheaded and unsettled. She hadn't fully recovered from the day's earlier episode, and she'd exerted too much, too fast.

But she did what she'd had to do. There was no other option but to protect Celina, no matter what.

Now the police had assured the people gathered in the tent city that the immediate danger was over, but that they all needed to wait inside their tents or other structures until they were led to the shelter at the high school in an orderly fashion.

But even forced by both her body and local law enforcement, Angela wasn't used to sitting still, especially not recently—not since the weather forecasts first put Port Provident in Hurricane Hope's crosshairs.

Pete Shipley, though, had no such issues. He arrived faster than she'd ever dreamed possible and once he got to their spot, he made quick work of everything that needed to be done, including gathering her limited possessions together and taking down the tent that had served as their temporary home the last few days.

Once everything had been removed from inside the tent, Angela and Celina came out and stood a few feet off to the side. Out of the corner of her eye, Angela could see a police officer keeping watch over them. Further in the distance, families were boarding school buses bearing the name of the district across the causeway, which made sense because all the buses belonging to Port Provident ISD had been flooded by the hurricane at the bus depot.

A strange sadness tugged at Angela's heart as she watched the fabric of the tent pool on the ground as Pete dismantled it. She knew the tent wasn't home—wasn't even close to a home—but it was surrounded by friends and neighbors. She and Celina were still right in the middle of the community they knew and loved. Everything else had changed, but that hadn't...until now.

Tonight's transfer of people out of the tent city would just speed up the plans of the government agencies and private groups to shepherd everyone to new locations—many would be off the island. When the red tape was all cut, and the rebuilding started, what would happen to the only neighborhood she and her daughter had ever known?

Would it look the same?

Would the character and the community of the island she loved so dearly ever look the same again?

"You ready? I've got everything loaded up, Angela." Pete stood a few paces away.

She wasn't ready. But she hadn't been ready for lots of other things in her life. She hadn't been ready to be a single mother, either. But she had done okay so far. Celina was happy and growing. She had to remember that God was in the details. The important thing now was to make sure she got healthy and they both stayed safe.

Angela would do anything for her daughter, whether she herself felt ready or not.

As Pete drove his truck back through the familiar streets of Port Provident, Angela was dogged with a feeling that she was on autopilot. Their route was more circuitous than it normally would have been, but it seemed like at least a block or two of every street was still closed, for one reason or another. Finally, they reached the main road, a two-lane highway that would take them out to East Provident Island, and the small clusters of beach neighborhoods.

She couldn't keep her eyes from looking at what the crisp moonlight illuminated all around her. In the few days since the hurricane hit, Angela's time had been consumed with checking on her constituents in and around the *La Missión* and Alamo Court neighborhoods, ensuring everyone was taken care of at the tent city, attending small gatherings at *La Iglesia* when she could, and making sure she took part in the unending stream of official meetings and updates which were required of her as a City Councilmember.

She'd been burning her candle at both ends--and a few spots in between.

She'd heard reports of East Provident's status from the city councilmember who represented their district, but she hadn't seen it for herself. There was more big debris out here, which made sense to her. There were lots of boats and boathouses, and the homes out here stood on stilts and most had storage areas underneath them. Lots of ice chests, fishing poles, and outdoor chairs and tables were strewn in the grass that divided the small four-lane highway.

And of course, wrapped around every pole and stuffed in every link of metal fencing was the drying seagrass. It was everywhere, washed up from the bottom of the ocean and left in the nooks and crannies when the waves pulled back. It looked like a giant thatched palapa had exploded and littered the once beautiful beachside landscape.

Angela noticed the silence behind her and turned her head to check on her daughter. Celina was asleep in the back seat, her head propped up by the headrest of her high-back booster seat that had been sitting inside the tent. The young girl looked so sweet, so untroubled. A lump pressed on the front of Angela's throat. She knew how much their world had changed, but she could only hope that Celina did not.

Angela blinked back tears as a prayer formed in her heart and flowed through her mind. *Please God, don't let her ever know. Don't ever let her know how much has changed. Don't let her childhood be scarred by this.*

Pete flicked on his blinker and made a left turn into Seagull Cove, a community of older beach homes. Angela had always loved this area. The homes were painted in a variety of cheerful colors. A light shone on a two-story teal house on the corner and caught Angela's eye, making the muscles in her cheeks twitch. She'd almost forgotten what it felt like to smile.

But then, the smile slipped away almost as soon as it appeared.

Pete turned into a driveway and pulled forward under the stilts of a faded green house with a large deck out front.

He looked behind him as he put the truck in park. "She crashed, huh?"

"Before we even hit the Open Water Highway. It's more than an understatement to say she's been out of her routine and off her schedule lately."

Pete nodded. "Then let's let her sleep."

"I can't just leave her out here, Pete."

"I didn't mean for you to leave her out here, Angela." He gave a short laugh as he hopped easily out of the truck. "I'll carry her in."

Angela opened the door and tried to get out as quietly as possible. "Are you sure you can get her?"

Pete handed her his keys as he laughed again, this time a rumbly laugh that echoed off the beams holding the little beach house about twelve feet off the ground. It amplified the sound and doubled the laughter. For the second time in less than five minutes, Angela thought about how much she missed laughter and smiles and a time, not so long ago, when things seemed easier.

"I have carried more than one pregnant woman in labor at the birthing center. I'm pretty sure I can get a what—five-year-old?" Pete opened the door to the back seat and gently leaned over Celina and unbuckled the seatbelt.

"She's six. And you did that like a pro. I always manage to wake her up when I unbuckle the seatbelt."

Pete slipped his arm behind Celina's neck and the other under her knees and with a deft twist had her seamlessly out of the car. As he turned back toward Angela, he grinned. "I guess I have the winning touch."

He had a winning smile, there was no doubt in her mind about that. It set her at ease, at least for this small moment.

"Can you unlock the front door, and bring up my bag out of the bed of the truck? I'll carry her in. I've got a guest room—I'll put her on the bed in there, then we can come back out and get your things."

Angela picked up Pete's blue bag and ran up the stairs ahead of him and Sleeping Beauty. Pete passed her, holding Celina, and another thing she hadn't realized she'd missed took up residence in her mind.

Cologne. She hadn't run across many men who didn't smell like sweat and drywall dust these days. But Pete Shipley smelled like bergamot and cinnamon. It had been almost six years since she'd been around a man that made her nose want to do a double-take and drink in his scent.

Pete's neighborhood made her smile, and his cologne made her long for a time so long ago she'd thought she'd forgotten it. She couldn't help but wonder what other surprises she was in for.

And now, she couldn't stop herself from thinking coming out here was a big mistake.

What on earth had she been thinking, leaving people she trusted— even though the idea of temporary shelter was precarious at best—to come out to the other end of the island with Dr. Pete Shipley, even if he was Gloria Rodriguez's boss, and there were few people whose instincts she trusted more than Gloria's? She'd battled her own blood sugar most of her life, she could have gotten through for another few days. Things would be better once the immediate stress settled down. Stress always aggravated her condition. Celina was scared of the shelter, but they'd have been together. It wouldn't have been like the night of the hurricane.

She could have calmed her daughter's fears.

Or at least she should have tried instead of picking up the phone and calling this doctor she hardly knew and whose smile was a distraction she hadn't counted on and didn't need.

Too late now. She'd just have to trust Gloria's skill in judging people and get a plan together to get out from under this roof as quickly as possible.

Angela placed the bag on the kitchen counter as they walked in the door. She followed a few paces behind Pete and watched as he transferred Celina to the guest bed. Her sweet girl didn't even stir a muscle as the doctor laid her down with practiced skill.

Angela breathed out and pushed the swirling threads of doubt and second-guessing out of her mind for a minute.

Celina. She'd done it all for Celina. Good or bad, she thought of Celina first and acted on what she knew her little girl needed.

Just like she'd done for the past six years.

Pete tiptoed across the doorway and closed the plain white door behind him with the softest of clicks. "Now, let's get you taken care of. One more quick check of your sugar, okay?"

Without even processing that she was taking the action, Angela froze. No one ever took care of her. She didn't need someone to take care of her. As soon as she had this sugar mess straightened out, she could take care of her sick daughter—and herself.

Just like always.

Pete followed her lead and hesitated as well. "Is something wrong, Angela?"

Her response, again, was instinct. She shook her head and held out her finger. "No. Go ahead."

Pete quickly did all the prep, lanced Angela's finger, and processed the test strip. The machine quickly went to work. His brow wrinkled a bit as he read the results.

"Okay then, why don't you just sit over there." Pete pointed the oversized chair, covered in a faded blue fabric, sitting under a bank of windows. "You can put your feet up on the table. Whatever makes you comfortable. I just want you to relax and take some of that load off your shoulders so your adrenaline can come down and we can help your body get your blood sugar stabilized."

Angela did as she was told, and sank into the corner of the

overstuffed chair. She leaned her head back just a little and realized she could see the edge of Provident Bay toward the end of the street.

"Really nice view you have here, even in the dark. I love the ripple of moonlight on the water there in the bay." If she focused on the gentle roll of the water, maybe she could be on the way to following the doctor's orders to lower the level of pounding in her veins and her head.

"It's the best." Pete rummaged through a succession of cabinets in the small kitchen. "The house is about thirty-five years old. It's not really much to look at, and the layout is a little wonky. I think the original owner built a little one-one camp house, and then other owners just added on as they wanted to. Clearly, there's not much of a plan. Or hallways, really. Sometimes I feel like the rooms are stuck on like Legos. But the minute I realized I could be on my front porch and see across the way to the ocean or be on my back porch and watch the sun set over the bay at the end of the street, I was sold. When I bought it, I had grand plans to fix the place up, but I guess that won't matter much now."

"What do you mean?" She pulled her stare off the waving of the marshy grasses around the edge of the bay.

Pete came into the living room. "Well, with the clinic closing, I'm hoping to get a position with Mercy Medical Mission and do some foreign medical work."

"So you're looking to leave Port Provident and sell the house?"

"Pretty much." He nodded and held out half a banana and a canister of mixed nuts. "Your sugar dropped back a little bit since I checked you earlier today, so I want it to come up just a little bit more. The half a banana is a more simple carbohydrate to bring your levels up a little more. Once we get you where I need you to be, the nuts are some good dense protein that should help stabilize things. We don't want you to go too high—slow and steady is the best prescription."

Angela put her phone on the small table beside her and reached for the banana, then took a deliberate bite. Pete put the container of nuts on the table as well, and they rattled slightly when the phone began to buzz.

"Angela Ruiz," she answered, hoping she didn't sound like she was talking with her mouth full.

"Angela, it's Marco." Her nephew, Marco, was the pastor at *La Iglesia de la Luz del Mundo*, the church which had long made up the backbone of the community in which she grew up and was now privileged to represent in city government. "Are you okay? I heard you got sick."

She knew the lightning-quick speed of the Port Provident grapevine. Apparently, even with the entire island in a state of total disarray, it still didn't miss a beat. "I'm fine. But how did you hear?"

"Well, that's why I called, although I'm sorry I'm calling so late. There's been so much going on today that this is the first moment I've had to myself. A man came by with a truck full of supplies. He said he stopped to see you, but you got sick before he could really talk to you. Then some of the others at the tent community directed him here to the church. So, I wanted to make sure you were okay, but also to see what you wanted me to do with all this."

The truck. She'd forgotten all about the truck of donations. She couldn't believe herself. When she'd seen the back of that utility truck, stuffed full with goods, she'd thought it was like manna from Heaven. And then she'd completely forgotten about it.

Momentarily, she feared God would think her ungrateful.

That certainly wasn't it, but she guessed it was time to admit she couldn't keep track of everything right now. "I honestly hadn't thought about it, Marco. You know how I get when my blood sugar gets off. Is there a place you can store it all at the church?"

"Well, we did get the carpet and such ripped out of the sanctuary this week, so I had them unload it back in that area back behind where the pulpit used to be. There's food, there's clothing, there's household goods, and even medical supplies. It's truly an answered prayer."

She could hear the joy in his voice. "I know. I'm glad they were directed to you. I can't make it to *La Iglesia* tonight, but how about I come tomorrow morning, and we'll make a plan for it?"

"*Bien.* I think we'll be able to do a lot of good. But I just don't know what the best approach is."

Angela didn't want to admit it, but the thought of having so much when right now there was so little was a bit overwhelming. The old adage said you had to eat an elephant one bite at a time, but when one elephant was all you had, you tended to wish that elephant could be all things to all people.

"We'll figure it out. I'll see you in the morning, okay?"

"*Bien*, Angela. See you then."

She disconnected the call and sighed lightly.

"What's wrong?" Pete sat lightly on the edge of the small table. He leaned forward, and when Angela looked, she could see nothing but compassion in them.

"Nothing's wrong, really. That truck of donated goods from earlier today was taken to the church. My nephew—who is actually older than me—is the pastor, and he needs me to come out in the morning and decide what to do with it all." She picked up her phone and scrolled through a few things. "But my calendar is out of control tomorrow. I've got meetings for most of the day. I thought I could make it first thing in the morning, but I just can't. And now that we're out here, I'm also going to have to ask you to drive us back into town early so I can find someone who can watch Celina for the day."

"No, you're not." Pete tapped the screen on his own smartphone and did a few quick swipes. "You do what you have to do. I can meet your nephew at the church and see what all has been donated and come up with a plan."

"That's not your job, Pete."

"My job?" He gave a dry laugh. "I'm a doctor. My job is taking care of my patients. And right now, you're my entire patient load. So my job is to make sure you reduce your stress level so you can keep your insulin levels maintained. Think of it as concierge medicine. They say that's the next big thing in healthcare, anyway."

A nagging sense of discomfort poked at her. "No, Pete, really. You've been more than generous. I can see why Gloria enjoyed working for you the last few years. But…"

He cut her off, and that sense of discomfort pricked even more firmly.

"But nothing, Angela. I don't have a job right now, until I hear back on what I hope will be my next opportunity. My time is my own, except for an appointment with a FEMA inspector at the end of the week to discuss some structural things at the clinic. You have too much on your plate right now, I don't have enough. I can't make city government decisions for you, but I can organize cases of water and diapers. My responsibility is to make sure you get well, and lowering your stress is one way to help you do that. I'm offering you two extra hands. Are you telling me you're not going to take them?"

She wanted to turn him down. She'd stood on her own two feet for a long time. She'd never needed to clone any part of herself before.

But two more hands sounded like a gift right now.

Angela picked up what was left of her banana and popped the last bite in her mouth. She could still feel her sugar levels bouncing around inside like a bobblehead doll. She didn't like admitting it, but Pete had been right earlier. She had to get well so she could take care of the people who depended upon her—an entire district of them.

Plus Celina. Even if she let Pete go do a preliminary evaluation of what had been brought to the church, she still had a responsibility to her daughter.

"I still have to find a place for Celina."

"She can come to the church. Your family is there, and all your church and neighborhood family too, right?" He reached out and patted her hand. If only every doctor had a bedside manner that was so equally decisive and caring.

"So we're settled?" Pete raised an eyebrow.

"I guess so. I don't think you're taking no for an answer." A wide yawn escaped Angela's mouth. For the first time in longer than she cared to remember, she felt tired not because of exhaustion, but because she'd relaxed. The thought of tomorrow didn't completely stress her out.

"Doctor's orders." Pete stood up from his chair. "Celina seemed perfectly healthy when I carried her up. I think she just needs a good night's sleep on a real bed and she'll be her regular self in the morning."

Angela agreed. Her sweet, compassionate girl worried about her mother more than she should. Her first real night of rest in a real bed in more than a week would probably do her more good than all the medicine in the world.

Pete pointed toward a door near the kitchen. "That's the bedroom. You can stay in there."

Angela looked around the rest of the small beach house. She didn't see any other doors. And the living room clearly gave off a "bachelor who wasn't home much" vibe.

"But what about you? Where are you going to sleep? You don't even have a couch in here."

He grinned, and this time Angela knew the flutters in her veins didn't come from glucose. "Out on the deck. I happen to know where there's a pretty good tent. I have an airbed in the closet, so I'll get everything set up out there, and then my house is your house."

"My tent?"

He nodded. The white teeth of his smile stood out brightly among the slightly-more-than-five-o'-clock shadow that dusted his cheeks and chin. "Why not? I've been camping before. The tent is in the bed of my truck. I'll just go down and get it. It was easy to take down. It shouldn't be any problem to put it back up."

Angela didn't even know what to say, except that she wasn't sure she could trust his planning abilities for tomorrow because his current plan for sleeping arrangements was nothing short of ridiculous. He was really planning on sleeping in a tent?

"But...couldn't you just put your airbed here in the living room?"

Angela knew he was a skilled doctor and had a compassionate bedside manner, but as he cocked that eyebrow again, the combination of it and his cheeky grin made her wonder just what sort of man Dr. Pete Shipley really was.

"Look, my allergies are a mess right now with all the stuff the storm has blown into the air, so I snore, okay? If you and Celina want a good night's sleep, you'll gladly take me up on my offer and put me out under the stars."

Angela had seen a lot of stars on their drive out to East Beach, their clear brightness twinkling above the water, undimmed by the sheer number of lights back in the core of the city. But as Dr. Pete Shipley gave her a quick wink to punctuate his assertion, Angela couldn't help but wonder if there wasn't something equally bright about this man who'd literally turned his life upside down and graciously opened his home to help a friend of a friend.

She could see now why Gloria had always spoken highly of her boss. Everyone needed a friend like Pete Shipley, even if the arrangement was only temporary.

The next morning, after he'd dropped Angela off at City Hall and settled Celina in with some family and friends gathered on the lawn of the church, Pete did a double-take at the sight of the mountain of generosity in front of him. Since Hurricane Hope, it had felt like Port Provident had been shut off from the rest of the world. But this was real, tangible proof that people off the island and around the world had heard about what had happened.

And more than that, it was proof that they cared.

Four teenagers had been dispatched to help him, and they spent the morning sorting the goods into piles. Food, clothing, and household goods each went to a separate corner of the torn-out sanctuary. Without carpet or fixtures, the room resembled a warehouse more than a house of worship.

Pete himself took responsibility for anything that could be classified as medical supplies. He'd found a pen and a notepad and started taking inventory of what they had. He still wasn't sure what they were going to do with all this, but it would be easier to pull together a plan once he knew exactly what he was dealing with.

It was kind of like putting together a diagnosis for stuff. And if there was one thing he remained confident in, it was his ability to put together a diagnosis.

He wasn't too sure about some other things in his life, but he was still a good doctor, so he figured he'd just focus on that for now.

"Dr. Pete! Dr. Pete!" The door at the back of the sanctuary opened with a crash, and the noise didn't stop. Celina ran up to him and tapped him on the back with a force that was more like a respiratory therapist trying to loosen some phlegm in the lungs.

She waggled a stuffed animal in his face. "They sent toys! They sent toys!"

"They sent a little bit of everything, didn't they?" Pete thought the light in her eyes could have illuminated the whole island.

"Can I have this one? Please?" She hugged the brown bear tightly. He was a squishy sort, with thick, glossy fur and rather pronounced ears.

Pete had wanted to get everything catalogued and a plan developed before letting anything leave the temporary storage setup here in the sanctuary. "Well, we need to figure out what we are doing with everything first."

He dropped to his knees so he could be eye-level with Celina as they talked.

"Oh." The one syllable sank to a low octave. "I just miss Huggy Lovey. A lot."

He'd remembered Celina mentioning that name yesterday, and his curiosity was piqued. "Who is Huggy Lovey?"

Celina looked at her shoes and scuffed them on the ground. "He was my stuffed dog. I used to cuddle with him at night. But we forgot and left him in my room, and Mama said he got all wet. I just want someone to snuggle with."

Pete nodded. He remembered that feeling of snuggling, remembered crawling up in the narrow hospital bed with Anna during those too-long, yet too-short three months of failed chemotherapy. He'd held her close and promised her he'd take away the pain if he could. As always, as soon as the regret squeezed his heart, he reminded himself that they'd stretched the boundaries of medicine as far as they could, but he wasn't God. None of his colleagues in the medical profession were.

He remembered thinking only a few short moments ago that at least he was a good doctor. As he pushed the memories of osteosarcoma and futility out of his mind, he tried to push away the self-doubt that crept into his mind too, even though he knew he wasn't an oncologist—and the very good ones Anna had did everything they could.

But this time, that gray cloud that pushed into his heart wouldn't leave. He missed holding someone so tightly that you could forget everything else around you.

"You can keep the bear," he said simply, giving an absent ruffle to the hair on Celina's head. He wished it had been that easy to hold on to his heart.

The petite, dark-headed little pixie twirled and skipped with her new bear, then ran off to show it to some of the older ladies of the church who were gathered outside.

"Dr. Shipley?" Pastor Ruiz walked into the sanctuary as Celina and the bear fluttered out. "It looks amazing in here."

Pete looked around the room and took in the transformation. He and his *ad-hoc* team had worked hard today to make sense of what had come their way. "I think we've made a good start. I am not quite sure what to do with it all exactly, yet, though."

"Are you ready for more?" He met Pete's eyes with a look of wariness, wrapped in a thin blanket of hope.

"More?" Pete wasn't quite sure what the pastor was getting at.

"Two more trucks are coming today. I just got off the phone with the pastor of one of our sister churches. They're apparently bringing furniture and some things like that as well. One of their members owns a regional furniture chain and decided to make a sizeable donation. Plus, several other members decided to clean out pieces they weren't using. I think we're going to have a full house, so to speak, by the end of the afternoon."

Pete looked around the room. He saw a lot of hard work and progress—he was proud of the order he'd been able to bring to the chaos in just a few hours. But in his mind's eye, he could see all the work still to be done at the clinic. He had gotten things pretty far along there, but he still had an obligation to get everything wrapped up and get the property on the market so he could be ready to move into the next phase of his life as soon as he got the call from Mercy Medical Mission.

"I can help out for the rest of the day, Pastor Ruiz. But I'm not sure how much I can commit to beyond that. I still have a few things I need to wrap up for myself and my clinic. But for today, I'm at your disposal."

The pastor reached out and clapped a hand on Pete's shoulder and gave it a lightning-quick squeeze. "I understand, *hermano*. Our entire church family is grateful for any time you have to give. We all have more to do than we have time to do it in these days. Wouldn't it be nice if we could multiply the hours in the day like Jesus multiplied the loaves and fishes?"

Again, thoughts of Anna flickered through Pete's mind. If only he could have multiplied time. If he could have, he'd have given himself and Anna the lifetime together they'd planned for, instead of the twelve, crazy, short, hectic weeks they'd wound up with after her diagnosis was confirmed.

Twelve weeks wasn't enough time with the woman you loved. Twelve weeks wasn't enough to have a wedding, or a family, or to grow old together.

Pete wasn't sure a lifetime would have been enough, either.

He shrugged, reflexively trying to dust off the thoughts and the what-ifs.

"Something troubling you, Dr. Shipley? I don't have a functioning church building anymore, but I do still have two good ears."

Pete hadn't been asked if he wanted to talk about Anna in several years. He hadn't needed to put up any defenses or excuses in a long time.

He was glad to see that reflex was still second nature. "No, no, I'm fine, Pastor. Just fine."

"Come with me." The pastor sidestepped piles of donations and led Pete to a window on the far side of the room. "Look out there. Do you see them?"

"Mmm-hmm." Pete nodded. About twenty people were gathered on the lawn of *La Iglesia de la Luz del Mundo*. Some were seated on metal folding chairs under a white utility tent, others were milling around. A handful of kids chased each other in circles around an area of the grass that had been cleared of debris. Pete saw Celina's dark ponytail bobbing behind her as she dashed with her friends. He smiled a bit as he saw her new bear firmly held against her body, secured in the crook of her elbow.

"They're here because they have nothing now. Some of them owned homes in the neighborhood, others lived in complexes that received government assistance. The common denominator now is that whatever their circumstances were before Hurricane Hope, it's all been swept away. Everyone out there is an equal. I don't know if there's anyone on this island who hasn't lost something."

"I don't disagree, Pastor Ruiz. But I'm still trying to work through in my mind how we handle all this fairly. If everyone needs something, we need to make sure the process is equitable."

"Not really, *Hermano* Shipley."

"You can just call me Pete, Pastor Ruiz. "Brother Shipley" sounds pretty formal. But I'm not following you. Are you saying you've already got people tapped for all this? I don't think that's fair at all."

The pastor shook his head, then turned to Pete with a genuine smile. "I was praying over all these donations late last night. As I stood here, a verse came to mind—Jeremiah 29:7. Do you know that one?"

Pete had spent a lot of time in Sunday school as a kid. He figured he could still sing the preschool classics like "Jesus Loves Me" and the little ditty about Zacchaeus being a wee little man and climbing in a sycamore tree with the best of them.

But he'd been away from regularly attending church for a long time now. College, then residency with shifts in a busy emergency room hadn't left much time for activities, especially after Anna got sick. And of course, when he came to Port Provident to shift professional gears and become the medical director of the birthing center so his uncle could transition into retirement, not only had there not been time to go to church, there really hadn't been the inclination.

He liked to blame it on the unpredictability of babies being born.

But if he was honest, it wasn't that at all.

"No, I don't know it, Pastor. What does it say?" Pete volleyed the conversation back over to Pastor Ruiz before he caught himself talking about things that were better left packed up in the past.

"'Seek the welfare of the city where I have sent you into exile, and pray to the Lord on its behalf, for in its welfare, you will find your welfare'." He looked out at his congregants on the lawn as he quoted. "We have a lot of needs right now. Obviously, people have lost their homes and their worldly goods. Many of them have lost their doctors and have medical needs and are concerned about how they're going to get their medicines and checkups and such now that the hospital is closed indefinitely. Others are concerned about their children since the schools are closed. Many are concerned about their jobs. There's not just one need we have here right now. And between you and me, Dr. Shipley—I mean, Pete— I don't know where to start."

Pete nodded. He knew that feeling of inertia the pastor was talking about all too well. "What's your gut feeling telling you to do?"

"Oh, I don't listen to it," the pastor said, with a push of his wrist through the air. "I go with my God feeling. Which means I need to do exactly what the verse says. Pray for the welfare of this city. Pray for what's best for Port Provident and the people who live here."

4

All night, Pete had turned over Pastor Ruiz's words, but he couldn't complete the simple request Pastor Ruiz had given him. The people of Port Provident didn't need his prayers—they didn't work. If they did, Anna would still be alive.

What he could offer his fellow residents was hard work in the time he had available to give them before he headed off to wherever Mercy Medical Mission chose to send him.

And so, here he was, back at *La Iglesia*, lifting boxes, organizing piles, and making up spreadsheets on his laptop to catalog everything that was filling the makeshift warehouse. So much had poured in from generous congregations around the state of Texas and beyond.

As he tucked the last pack of diapers on the top of a large, wobbly pile, Pete's stomach let out a low rumble. He caught a glimpse of his watch. It was close to two in the afternoon. No wonder his stomach was causing a scene.

He knew the ladies of the church had been cooking on the front lawn earlier, using camp stoves and just about every other portable means of cooking. They'd been serving hot meals three times a day for the church members who had turned the grassy area in the southwest corner of the lawn into an unofficial gathering place to receive support and prayers from friends…and to hear the latest scoop on the community and the recovery.

He didn't have much to offer in the way of scoop or prayers, and his support was shown in the piles and rows of organized donations inside the sanctuary, but he hoped that the ladies could spare him a tortilla or two.

"Hi, Mrs. Garcia." Pete waved as he walked up to Gloria's mother. "Is there any lunch to spare?"

"*Pedro*," she said, dragging out the two syllables of his given name in Spanish. "I've told you before to call me Juanita. *Señora* Garcia is my mother-in-law. Don't make me any older! I'm already an *abuela* now. I'm still adjusting to having a granddaughter!"

"You know you love it, Juanita." She chuckled as Pete gave her name as much emphasis as she'd offered his, and punctuated it with a big grin. Gloria had long been one of his favorite people to work with, and over the years, he'd gotten to know her family as well. He'd been there when her sister Gracie delivered Gabriella— Juanita's beloved granddaughter. And when he was too tired to cook, he always stopped in at Juanita and Carlos' restaurant, *Huarache's*, where they always had a hot, home-cooked meal waiting. They always treated him with so much love and hospitality.

He'd miss them all when he left town. He probably only had a few weeks left to soak up the friendship of the good people in Port Provident he cared about, like the Garcia family…and the meals they cooked.

"Those tortillas look homemade. Could you maybe spare two? When Medical Mercy Mission sends me off to some corner of the world, I may not be able to get food like this. I think I need to double up." He looked up from the griddle and gave Juanita another smile as they made eye contact. "You know, for the memories."

"Do you know when you're leaving yet?" Juanita ladled a generous spoonful of rice on a disposable foam plate, next to an equally generous spoonful of beans.

"No, I'm still waiting on the official word that everything is a go, plus there are a few more things to do with the clinic before I move on."

"Gloria said you're selling the building and everything." She handed Pete the plate, loaded full of more food than he could have ever expected. "Let me get you a fork and spoon too."

"I am, Juanita. I won't be here to supervise any rebuilding—that's a long-term project, and I don't want to be a long-distance landlord, either. My uncle wants to stay retired, and so we both think the best thing to do is to clean it out, continue to navigate the insurance process, and let someone who is going to be here to invest in the Port Provident recovery do something new with it. It's in a great location, and being a historic home with a really nice layout, it's got a lot of potential."

Juanita nodded. "*Sí.* But we will miss having a doctor like you in the community."

"I've got a lot of great memories of my time here. I know I'll miss a lot of folks, too."

Pete started to scope out a place to sit. There were a few lawn chairs that seemed to be unoccupied. As though reading his train of thought, Juanita pointed toward a blue-and-white webbed chair near a large palm tree in the corner.

"Do you think you could go sit over there by Mrs. Escobar? She's been very worried about some medical things and how she's going to get her medicines since Provident Medical is expected to be closed for a while. Maybe you could talk with her and ease her mind a little bit?"

He didn't quite know what to say. He didn't have any insight into what was going on at Provident Medical, and since Mrs. Escobar had passed retirement age a long time ago, he felt pretty certain she didn't need advice on delivering babies, which was his specialty these days. But to say anything other than yes would not only be rude, it would be practically spitting in the face of the spirit of support and recovery that was wrapping around the island in the days since people returned home and started to assess what it would take to rebuild their future.

"Sure, Juanita. I don't know if I have any good advice to give, but I'll do what I can." Pete looked gratefully down at the hot, homemade meal in his hands. Sitting by Mrs. Escobar seemed to be the least he could do.

Juanita took off her apron and hung it from the end of the metal shelf behind her that had been set up as storage for the makeshift outdoor kitchen then she walked to a nearby cooler and plucked out a bottle of water. "*Bien.* I'll come with you. My tired old bones need a break anyway."

The group of five ladies buzzed with quick Spanish chatter between them as Pete and Juanita lowered themselves into the empty chairs at the edge of the semi-circle. Juanita jumped right in. Pete knew quite a bit of Spanish and was able to hold his own in conversations with patients, but he realized that right now, he could either turn all his concentration to following the six ladies as they spoke between and over one another or he could focus on tortillas, rice, beans, and some fresh mango slices.

With almost no hesitation, he chose the tortillas.

Halfway through his second tortilla, in mid-chew, the conversation turned Pete's way.

"I used to check my blood pressure every day, but now that everything in my home is gone, I don't have my monitor anymore. The hospital is closed, and my doctor is on the mainland now. I can't get over the causeway every day for a blood pressure check, and I don't know what to do."

Pete could hear the worry in Mrs. Escobar's voice. Before taking over the clinic, he'd been an ER physician. He knew all too well that many patients were fine with the day-to-day management of their conditions, but when changes came to their routines, it made many of them feel unsettled and out of control.

"I can help you with that. I have my bag of supplies in the trunk of my car, and I have everything I need in there to check your blood pressure," Pete replied. It would be simple to put this woman's mind at ease.

One of the other ladies spoke up. She was a type-two diabetic and wanted to check her sugar and was nervous because she was running low on her prescription. Another had stress headaches and just wished she could get her hands on a bottle of ibuprofen.

Pete finished his meal quickly and stood. "Give me a few minutes to get some things out of my car and get set up inside, then you can meet me in the sanctuary, and I'll be able to help all of you."

As he walked off, he caught more of the group's animated chatter —and he was pretty sure Mrs. Escobar said something about needing to fix him up with her granddaughter so she'd have a doctor in the family.

Pete chuckled to himself. He could check Mrs. Escobar's blood pressure, but for the other issues of the heart, she was on her own. A small twitch in his own heart came as he thought of Anna. He wasn't getting fixed up with anyone. He'd loved, and he'd lost.

And he wasn't ever planning on doing either again.

Angela waved goodbye to Libby Rawlings, the city councilmember for East Provident, who'd given her a ride back to Pete's beach house. She couldn't believe the sun was already starting to sink in the western sky, casting an intense orange glow on the water of Provident Bay down at the end of Pete's street.

A stillness hung in the air, and Angela breathed in deeply. Running from one meeting to another for the last twelve hours, she hadn't felt still all day.

And that was to say nothing of the restlessness in her soul. She had to get a plan together for a more permanent place for her and Celina to stay. Pete had been nothing but generous, but she wasn't about to make Pete sleep out on his porch again, no matter what he said about his snoring.

Oh, how she missed normal.

But she'd missed her daughter today too. And while she couldn't fix all the issues on the island, she could give her daughter a hug, and that would fix a lot of the unrest in her heart.

Angela walked up the outside stairs and crossed the wide deck that made up the front of the house, then knocked on the door.

"Mama!" As soon as the door cracked open, Celina wedged herself through the open space and threw her arms around Angela's waist.

"*Querida!*" Angela ruffled Celina's hair as she greeted her with a favorite term of endearment. "It smells amazing in here. Is that spaghetti?"

"It is." Pete stood a few feet away, stirring a few shakes of dried oregano into a bubbling pot of tomato sauce.

In the overhead light, Angela noticed a dash of gray running throughout Pete's closely-trimmed hair. In all the hectic ups and downs of yesterday, she hadn't really looked closely at Pete. She'd always been distracted, trying to do too many things at once. Part of dealing with the aftermath of a disaster and taking shelter in a makeshift refugee camp was that you didn't notice details anymore. Life became a task list. You checked one box, then moved on to another.

Since Hurricane Hope came to town, everything in Angela's life had been about survival—both hers and Port Provident's—not about details or the little things.

But right now, in her moment of slow sunglow and the peace she'd found in her daughter's warm hug, Angela forced herself to continue to press pause and just take in the moment. Strictly on the connection between friends, this man had opened up his home and his kitchen to her little family. Community and compassion were alive and well in Port Provident, and this evidence of that fact gave her strength for the road ahead.

"I really don't know how I can thank you," Angela said with simple gratitude.

Pete put the lid back on the saucepan. "It's just spaghetti. Not a big deal."

Angela wanted to say something more, but couldn't think of a way to describe her gratitude in a way that didn't come across as awkward.

Then Celina began to tug on her hand and the moment passed. "Pete! Can we show her? Please?"

"I have a feeling you're not talking about pasta." She tried to dislodge her hand from Celina's excited, pinching grip. "What is it?"

"I can't tell you unless Pete says so. It's a surprise." Celina's grip got stronger. If Pete didn't give the green light, Angela feared she might lose her thumb.

Pete clicked off both burners he'd been using on the stove. "Sure, kiddo. Celina and I worked at the church until after lunchtime, then we came back here and worked on a project together."

Celina began to drag her mother toward the door. "Come on, Mama!"

She flung open the door, let go of Angela's hand, and then took off at a sprint across the deck and down the stairs.

"Where are we going?" Angela questioned Pete as he closed the front door behind them.

"You'll see," he said, with a mischievous twinkle in his eye. Angela caught the white sparkle of the light and thought it complimented the salt in his light brown hair perfectly. It felt somehow disloyal to her constituents to be thinking of anything other than how to get their lives back to normal, but at the same time, it felt almost soothing to be thinking about something other than the aftermath of the hurricane.

Pete stopped at a plain door among the stilts which lifted the beach house more than ten feet off the ground. It was slightly hidden behind the garage area.

"Open it, Mama! Open it!" Celina couldn't keep her feet on the ground. She bounced with excitement. Angela couldn't think of anything that would get her daughter that excited, except maybe having Huggy Lovey back.

She reached her hand out slowly and put it on the doorknob. The orange light from earlier filtered through the spaces in between the boards of the deck and made a pattern on the dirt and concrete here below the house.

"Go ahead. Nothing in there will bite." Pete gave a little chuckle.

She turned the knob, then Celina gave the door a strong shove, pushing it wide open. Angela looked around. She saw a small kitchenette with a narrow, rectangular window across the room. Closer to her were two chairs and an older-model television on a low stand. Behind that area was a double bed covered in a blue and maroon patterned quilt with a large brown teddy bear sitting in a place of honor atop two white pillows. She recognized it as the guest bed Pete had laid Celina on last night when they'd arrived at her house. A small walled off area with a plain white door was tucked in the corner, which based on the layout, was probably a small bathroom.

It looked like an efficiency apartment—sparsely, yet fully furnished.

"What do you think?" Pete leaned against the door frame. "I'd moved the furniture upstairs when the storm came through and had just moved it all back down here about two days ago after scrubbing out the mud on the floors. It's hard to believe, but there wasn't much damage down here. This room was built to handle some flooding. Celina helped me clean—she's great with a mop—and my next door neighbor helped me move the guest bed down here. I had a twin-sized bed in here before the storm, but I knew that wouldn't work for the two of you, so I made a switch."

Angela didn't know what to make of the goosebumps popping up on the skin of her forearms. "But what is all this?"

"Well, Brownie the Bear needed a good home." Pete shrugged. The half-cocked smile never left the corners of his lips.

His answer left her with another question. Nothing really made sense. "Who is Brownie the Bear?"

"Mama! Brownie's right there on the bed." Celina gave the direct and obvious answer, in true six-year-old fashion.

"I see that. But where did Brownie come from, and why does he need an apartment?"

"Brownie came from the good people at the First Cornerstone Church of Spring, Texas. They're the ones who sent that truck yesterday. Brownie was on it, and he and Celina became fast friends. And Brownie needs a place to crash because Celina needs a place to crash. They're pretty inseparable." Pete's smile morphed into a full ear-to-ear grin. "And Brownie said he can't live in a tent. Humidity isn't good for his fur."

"Isn't it great, Mama? We can stay with Pete! We don't have to go back to the shelter or the tent!" Celina gave a little bounce and followed it up with a twirl.

The goosebumps had multiplied and turned into one big lump in Angela's throat. "No, really, we can't. I told you, this just had to be temporary. I can't take advantage of things my constituents don't have available to them. It's just not right."

"Not right?" The smile fell from Pete's face. He looked at her with a practiced seriousness, as though he were giving her a diagnosis she didn't want to hear. "I think you can get a lot more done for your people here. You'll have a space to work, and your daughter will feel safe and secure. You're not taking advantage of anything. You're not pulling any strings. You're not giving me anything in return. I'm offering this of my own free will. Well, that and because I have a soft spot for teddy bears who need a good roof over their heads."

Celina walked to the bed and grabbed Brownie. "Why can't we stay, Mama? This place is perfect. It's like a hotel."

Angela looked out the narrow window in the kitchen. The orange light had faded to a dull golden glow. Just like the light, things changed. Maybe she needed to give a little too. Maybe Pete was right. With a quiet place to go over paperwork and make notes, she could cut through the red tape faster and get together the plans and approvals she needed to make temporary housing—not emergency shelters or refugee tent communities—a reality for people all over Port Provident.

She felt a tug at her heart. The light was fading and taking her doubts with it. "Okay. We can stay. Just until we get the temporary housing situation worked out. Then we'll go with everyone else."

Celina ran and gave her another big hug, this time complete with additional stuffed bear love. "Thank you, Mama! Thank you! Brownie loves you too."

The smile on Celina's faced pushed the rest of Angela's lingering objections away. She hadn't seen her little girl this happy since before the storm. Even though their stay here would be temporary, maybe just the stability of four walls and a bed would help reassure Celina that everything would be okay.

And maybe knowing that there were generous people out there like Pete Shipley who just wanted to help and asked for nothing in return would help reassure Angela that everything would be okay, too.

Celina had asked to play with a fitness-themed game on Pete's video game console, so he'd gotten her set up, and she was bouncing and running and wiggling in the front part of the living room. She was burning off energy and also that fear that Pete had seen trailing her like Linus Van Pelt's blue blanket—only in this case, it was an *in*security blanket.

Her enthusiasm made Pete smile. And Pete had plenty of enthusiasm of his own right now. While he and Celina had been working downstairs earlier today, an idea had begun to take shape in his head.

It had all come together now, and he wanted to run it by Angela. He hadn't known her long, but he knew she cared about the people of Port Provident, and her opinion meant a lot to him as he decided whether or not to move forward with his idea.

"So I've been thinking," Pete said after the last strand of spaghetti had been eaten, and the dishes had been washed.

"About what?" Angela pulled some papers out of the bag she'd brought home with her.

"About the people at *La Iglesia.*"

She looked over the tortoise-shell frame of the pair of glasses she'd just slipped on for reading. The glasses framed her face, bringing boldness to her features. "You've got my attention. What about the people at *La Iglesia?*"

Pete sat down on the coffee table, next to Angela's overstuffed canvas bag, full of briefs and reports. "I've spent the last two days organizing all those donations, and I haven't known exactly what to do with them after I got them organized. But this afternoon, Gloria's mom introduced me to some of the women at the church, and they all had small health needs. I spent an hour after lunch checking blood pressure, handing out ibuprofen tablets and counseling them on what to do while everything is in limbo and their regular doctors are gone."

"I'm sure they appreciated that." A soft smile curved her lips. For the first time since he'd met her, Angela's face was free of worry. No furrow in the brow, no tightly pursed lips. She had relaxed, and it made Pete stop and give her more than just a passing glance. He wanted to do a double-take. But he didn't want to get caught staring, so he forced his eyes to look out the window to the stars twinkling over the bay.

"I think we could do more."

"We?"

"Well, mostly me. But it would be great to have your backing and to have people in the community know you support it. They think a lot of you in that neighborhood and that congregation, you know. I'm an outsider. But in the time I've got left here on Port Provident, I want to help. I still have some obligations with my own clinic, as you know, but I think I can find a balance. I think I can make a difference."

Angela leaned forward and placed the papers she'd been holding on top of the bag next to Pete. Her long brown hair brushed slightly against his leg as she shifted her position forward, then back.

"Tell me about it."

"I think we set up a place where people can come and shop for what they need, except there's no bill at the end. We set it up like a store and let people get what they feel is most meaningful to them. We can set values on certain types of items, and then let people take up to a value limit per day. It saves us from having to set up rules and systems that miss the mark. It puts a little structure around it and keeps people from cleaning everything out, yet still lets them have free access to what's been donated and what they feel like they need. I've been scratching my head, trying to figure out what would be an equitable way to divide all of the donations. But maybe it's not equity people need, it's…"

"Grace?" Angela picked up where Pete trailed off. "Not what they deserve, but what they need?"

She completed his train of thought perfectly, and he jumped back in with full agreement. "Exactly. Grace. That's what we can call it. The Grace Space."

Angela's maple syrup-colored eyes caught fire. He saw the moment the spark landed in them and got the life-puff of oxygen that made the color combust with golden embers.

"I love it," she said, nodding in enthusiastic approval. "So you'd set it up at the church? In the sanctuary?"

"I think that's the best place for right now. Pastor Ruiz said it would be weeks before they were able to start renovating the sanctuary. So it's a very functional, open space. But I want it to be more than a store. I want to set up a clinic area too."

"A clinic area? How so?" Once again, Angela leaned closer, and Pete enjoyed the shared excitement that ran between them. The days had been long and joyless after Hurricane Hope. It felt good to feel good about something again.

Pete laid out his vision for the clinic, using his medical connections and leaning on residents from Provident Medical Center's world-class medical school. He felt confident he could even get some screening trucks from a hospital in Houston and perhaps a mobile pharmacy van from an independent pharmacy near Rice University that he had strong ties with.

"As we're talking, it's coming together in my head even more clearly."

The soft smile maintained residence on Angela's lips. "So when do you think you can have it up and running?"

"Two or three days. I just need to make a few phone calls."

"Ok, what else?" Angela reached inside her bag and pulled out a notepad and a red pen. "How can I help?"

"I need a few more people to help me organize according to the new plan in my head, but I should be able to find those at the church. Do you think you could get the relief agencies to set up some mobile offices in the parking lot to help people fill out paperwork? It would be nice to have a one-stop-shop."

Angela scribbled on the notepad. "It definitely would. Now if I could get FEMA to get me an answer on this temporary housing site."

"What temporary housing site?"

Angela leaned back in the chair and watched Celina do a very animated dance to a pop song that had become popular toward the beginning of the summer.

"I've been working on getting the permits to turn the school softball and baseball fields into an area where FEMA can bring in trailers for temporary housing—like they did after Katrina in Louisiana and Mississippi, and lots of other places." She tucked her hair behind one ear with a forceful swoop of frustration. "They've turned down several options because of elevation and floodplain restrictions. Today, I got a memo that said that the fields are also considered a coastal high hazard area, and they won't put the infrastructure and trailers in there now. So I'm back at square one."

"What about the RV park a few blocks from Provident Medical, as you're headed toward those brown apartments?"

Angela turned and faced Pete squarely. "I know the place you're talking about. But I'm not sure what you're getting at."

"I know the guy who owns it. I've helped deliver both of his kids. They closed two weeks before the hurricane, right after Labor Day weekend, when the tourist season ended. He and his wife are about to put the park on the market now because they have to move closer to her parents to help with some health issues. Do you want me to give him a call and see if maybe the city could use it in the interim? I don't see a whole lot of buyers lining up for anything like that in Port Provident right now."

"Oh my goodness, Pete, would you? That's a great idea. If the elevation checks out and they'll let the city use it, we could get people in there so quickly because they've already got the water and sewer and electrical infrastructure built in."

Angela's excitement propelled her to move like a flash. She jumped out of her chair, leaned over and gave Pete a quick hug. He felt her arms go around his shoulders, as smooth as a narrow ribbon of silk.

She pulled back as quickly as she'd jumped and gave Pete a sheepish glance through thick black lashes. "Sorry about that."

Pete could still feel an echo of her light, quick hug around the top of his forearm, just below the joint. He wasn't quite sure what to make of that sensory memory, but he knew he didn't want Angela to apologize. He hadn't felt a lightning-quick ripple of emotion like that since he'd first met Anna. The recognition that his pulse moved a little faster at the feel of Angela's skin making contact with the thin cotton of his shirt scared him a little. He hadn't ever expected to observe that particular fleeting change of heart rate ever again.

But on the other hand, it proved he wasn't as hollow inside as he felt most days. And that knowledge scared him a little bit more. But he didn't want Angela to know any of what he was thinking. Pete forced himself to regroup and act like nothing had piqued his pulse.

"Sorry for what? Excitement? Angela, a lot has gone wrong lately. It's okay to be excited when something goes right."

Like when an unexpected embrace makes you take notice. Pete pushed the thought from his mind again, trying to focus on the discussion at hand. He didn't need to answer these questions as they related to Angela. They were both caught up in the excitement of seeing their plans get underway. That was it and nothing more.

"I know, but..." she fidgeted a little as she settled back in the armchair.

Pete hadn't known her long, but he liked her fire. She was passionate about those she cared for. Her eyes had lit up like syrup over a hot flame when she'd caught the same vision he'd had for The Grace Space. He felt like he understood this need she had to do for others what they couldn't do for themselves. He had the same need, but in his line of work, it was called a passion for healing. Either way, he recognized the same force in her which propelled his need to quickly get to work at wherever Mercy Medical Mission wanted to send him.

"But nothing. You're going to help me see that the vision for The Grace Space becomes a reality. I get to help you with your project. It all works together."

"Don't get me wrong, Pete. I'm grateful that you have the

connections to help. But you've already done so much. You've opened up your home to my daughter and me and mucked out a studio apartment so she'd have a place to feel safe and call her own." Angela paused, and the far-off look in her eyes made it clear she was choosing her words carefully. "I've just been on my own for a while now. I'm not used to asking others for help."

"It's not a sign of weakness, you know."

She met his gaze, and he could see the slow fade of the golden glints that had been in her irises only moments before. "I know. I've just been disappointed by people too many times, I think. I'm used to things not working out."

Angela cast a deliberate look over her shoulder, and the smile that had been on her lips twisted with an edge of wryness.

Pete knew she was a single mom. But now he could clearly see there was more to the story. He wanted to ask, like a doctor gathering a medical history with a new patient. But before he could decide how to ask, Angela stood up.

"Come on, *Querida* Celina. It's time for bed. Let's go down to our apartment and get your bear."

Angela picked up her bag and papers and gently herded her still-dancing daughter toward the door. As she passed, Celina bumped playfully into Pete and wrapped her arms around his waist for a hug.

"Thanks for being my friend, Dr. Pete. It's good to have a friend like you."

Pete returned the hug and promised himself that he'd be that friend for Celina...and her maple-eyed mother.

*P*ete could hear the stress in Angela's voice as she called him quickly during a break in meetings. "This meeting between FEMA and the city and your friends is taking longer than I thought it would. We're making progress, and I think we'll be able to get the negotiations finished today, but I probably won't be back at the apartment until after dinner. I hate to impose, but can Celina join you for dinner?"

"I brought her home with me from the church. She's dancing with that game again right now while I finish up the last few details we need to open The Grace Space officially at the end of the week."

"So it's really coming together quickly?" Her voice took on a slightly higher pitch, a glimmer of hope breaking through the stress.

"It is. I've gotten so much cooperation from my contacts at Provident Medical and the medical school plus the people on the mainland that I contacted. Everyone wants to feel useful right now, and this is giving them a great chance to help out and use their skills."

"Sounds wonderful. Maybe between your project and mine, we can finally get things moving on the island and bridge that gap between disaster and whatever normal is going to look like here going forward."

She paused, and Pete could hear voices in the background. "I have to go—our break is over. But thank you for watching Celina this evening. I guess I owe you again."

Pete didn't need to be thanked for spending time with Celina. The little girl had bloomed practically overnight. He could barely believe that the dancing, singing rockstar in front of him was the same clingy, wary girl he'd met only a few days ago.

"You don't owe me anything," he said, while his mind slipped back to that lightning-quick embrace she'd given him last night. It had been a long time since an unexpected emotion had jumped through his being. If he could collect anything in return from Angela, it might be another opportunity to know, even for a short moment, he could still feel.

Angela said goodbye and hung up. Pete stared at the phone in the palm of his hands. He'd always thought there'd never be enough time to process all he'd lost when he lost Anna. But if he was honest, he'd now lost his job and place of employment and much of the town he currently called home. He was determined to rebuild those things, to envision life differently—not as a doctor delivering babies, but as a doctor doing meaningful work on behalf of people around the world who had nothing. He could see his life moving from Port Provident to some far-flung corner of the world. He had embraced the idea of leaving the clinic behind and setting up shop in a tent or some other mobile clinic.

If he could envision all of that, why couldn't he envision his emotions differently?

He didn't have the answer. And part of him didn't like that a two-second hug and a brush of hair from last night had him questioning all of this. He tried to steady all of the forts he'd built around his heart just to keep moving after he realized there'd be no wedding to Anna and there'd be no happily ever after. He wasn't ready for those barriers to crack or crumble.

Pete looked from the phone to Celina. He didn't have the answer to these more significant emotional questions about where his future might lead, but he did have a box of microwaveable quick-cooking mac and cheese in the kitchen and some fishing poles down in the garage.

Besides, he reassured himself, he didn't have to have the answer because in a few weeks it would all be a moot point anyway. He'd go to wherever Mercy Medical Mission was sending him, and he'd never have to see the multi-colored look of warm maple syrup in Angela Ruiz's eyes again. He wouldn't have to question why he cared about how he felt last night when her arms flung around his shoulders.

"Hey, Celina?"

She stopped her dance of perpetual motion at the sound of his question.

"Hey, Dr. Pete. What's up?"

"Have you ever been fishing?"

Her eyes grew as large as those on the sand trout he soon hoped to be catching. "No, never. Mama doesn't really like slimy things, and fish are kinda slimy."

Pete chuckled. "That they are, Celina. But they're also pretty tasty. What do you think of some quick mac and cheese and then we can walk down to the end of the street and see what we can find out in the bay?"

Celina nodded, a much more satisfactory answer to a much more important question than anything else he'd been wondering in the past few minutes.

The bobbing of the water had always soothed Pete's soul. But he had no idea how much seeing a simple fishing trip through a child's eyes could make him smile as well.

Celina loved everything about their fishing adventure. She wanted to look in the marsh grass and see small minnow-sized fish hiding in between the blades. She stood at the water's edge, looking studiously for crabs or other meandering crustaceans. She even made up a song that consisted liberally of the line "Hey, fishy fishy! Come and swim on by!" sung over and over.

There was late day sun, a gentle breeze that ruffled the hair which stuck out below his baseball cap, and a sense of peace that he hadn't felt since long before the storm.

Pete took a half-step back and raised his arm, then cocked it back and cast his pole. The line curved in a perfect parabola and landed right in the deepest part of this small finger that marked the border of the Seagull Cove community.

Now to wait for the tug of a fish at the other end of the line, which was perfect, because for right now, Pete felt like he had all the time in the world.

"Pete! I thought that was you. But who's this?" Dr. Gordon Patterson and his black Labrador retriever slowed as they came around the curve of the sidewalk. Dr. Patterson was chief of the division of Maternal-Fetal Medicine at Provident Medical, and he'd become a mentor to Pete during the years Pete had run the birth center at the edge of the large teaching hospital's shadow.

"Hey, Gordon. This is Celina Ruiz. Her mother is City Councilwoman Angela Ruiz. I'm watching her for a bit this afternoon while her mother is in a meeting with FEMA and the city regarding temporary housing arrangements."

Gordon gave the leash a little slack so his dog could sniff at the edge of the marsh grass, not too far from Celina's perch. "I heard they had to move everyone back to the shelter at the high school."

"There was a shooting. Angela and Celina actually came to stay in my downstairs apartment after that."

Gordon nodded. "A shelter is no place for a child. She looks like she's enjoying Provident Bay life just fine."

Pete gave the pole a gentle pop to keep the line moving and hopefully catch the eye of an interested fish. "Most definitely. I'll definitely miss it myself, once I'm gone."

"Heard anything back yet?"

"No, but I'm expecting something any day now. I was told it was just a matter of getting some things moved around and then finding a slot to put me in. It's more or less a done deal."

"So, how long are you going to be gone for?" Gordon adjusted his sunglasses as the sun shifted a bit in the sky.

"I don't know. I don't really have a timeframe. As long as they need me, I guess. But with all the heartache around the world, I guess they'll always need me." Pete gave a bit of a shrug. He hadn't given too much thought to coming back, just to going.

"Well, you can't stay forever, Pete. Or you'll miss out on moments like this." The older man pointed at Celina, studying the crawl of a crab in the muddy shallows.

Pete turned slowly and looked back at his mentor. Gordon gave a little wave. "Well, I guess you could definitely get married and have a family anywhere in the world. Just whatever you do or wherever you go, don't isolate yourself. Work can do that to you. I was so focused on medical school, residency, fellowships, the pursuit of excellence in medicine that I lost track of a whole other track of my life. I lived to work. I didn't work to live. When I married Olivia, I was past forty. When we started having kids, I was forty-five. I'd spent so many years thinking of my job first that when I realized Liv was the one thing in my life I couldn't do without—well, nobody likes to say this, but I had some regrets about how I'd prioritized things over the years. However, I used the opportunity to take a hard look at myself and where I was going, and I think I've got it right. There's a balance there, and I wouldn't have missed this second phase of my adult life for the world."

Woof. Gordon's dog let out a low, bass rumble.

"Enjoy the fishing Pete. It was good to see you—it's been too long. No matter where you wind up, don't be a stranger, okay?" The dog let out another woof, as punctuation to his owner's sentence. Gordon gave the leash a quick tug and took a step. "It sounds like he's ready to go."

"It does indeed. Good to see you too, Gordon."

Pete watched the dog trot ahead, as far as his leash would allow him to go. Gordon was right. The dog was ready to go. And until this very moment, Pete had been ready to go too. He shifted his gaze from the black Lab back to the little girl who had made the afternoon so fun and full of memories.

He'd once talked of marriage and family like it was a given in his life. Then those dreams had been pulled away, and he'd refocused his life and his goals in the wake of unexpected tragedy.

Pete couldn't deny—didn't want to deny—that he'd been called to serve others. But as he'd baited Celina's hook and pointed out crabs and little fish to Celina, he also couldn't deny something had stirred way down in the bottom of his heart. Something he thought he'd packed away forever.

And he hadn't seen Gordon in months, so it couldn't have been a coincidence that he just happened to be walking his dog on this stretch of sidewalk by the bay and drew the conclusion about the afternoon that Pete had been hesitant to draw for himself.

He'd just wanted to create some memories for Celina—every kid on an island needed to know the joy of casting a line in the water.

But had he unexpectedly created some questions for himself?

Angela had finally gotten her car out of the parking garage where she'd left it during the storm. Now that she was commuting between Seagull Cove and downtown Port Provident, she needed it again. Once she'd made it back to Pete's, she parked her car between the pilings of the beach house, near the door to her temporary downstairs apartment home. She climbed the stairs and went to the door and knocked, eagerly anticipating one of Celina's all-encompassing hugs.

But there was no answer. And strangely, she didn't hear any noise from the other side of the door, either. No danceable pop music was blaring from the TV and no sounds of dinner, like the clink of silverware on a plate.

Angela's breath came short. Pete had said he would take care of her little girl and feed her dinner. How stupid could she be to assume that meant they'd stay at the house. How stupid could she be to leave her daughter completely alone—without at least the watchful eyes of the *abuelas* at *La Iglesia*—with someone she barely knew.

She would have kicked herself, but that would take time away from digging in her purse for the key to the beach house that Pete had given her. She found it in the corner of the zippered pocket at the back of the bag, and with a slight tremble in her fingers, she forcefully pushed the key into the lock and turned.

The door opened and revealed that she'd been right. The house was empty. Angela felt a boulder avalanching through her chest as her heart pounded wildly out of control.

Where were they?

Where was her precious Celina?

Quickly, she ran through the house, looking for any clues to where they might have gone, but nothing seemed out of the ordinary or out of place. In the corner of the living room, she stopped. Placing her hands on her hips to steady herself, Angela looked out the window blankly, racking her brain for some idea of what to do.

A car driving past on the street below caught her attention. Her eyes followed as it headed for the bend at the end of the street. As the red sedan rounded the curve, Angela noticed two people sitting atop a concrete picnic table underneath a flat metal shelter. A baseball cap mostly covered the hair on one head, but she could see a mix of brown and premature silver mixing under the edge of the white cap. The other head was covered in thick black hair, held in a sturdy ponytail high atop the crown of the skull.

As she waited for her breathing to flutter back down to a more normal rate, she watched the scene below. Pete pointed up at a seagull cruising past on the breeze. Celina leaned toward Pete as though she were saying something. Pete tipped his head back laughing, and put his arm easily around Celina's shoulders and gave it a gentle squeeze.

Moments before, Angela would have sprinted to the ends of the earth to find her baby. Now, she stood in the corner of Pete's small living room, rooted to the hardwood flooring below her feet as she took in the full scene.

Fishing poles rested against the side of the picnic table, and a tackle box sat nearby. Angela could see the back-and-forth of little tennis shoes as her daughter's feet swung happily off the edge of the table.

But most of all, Angela saw something she'd never before seen in Celina's life—the glimpse of a father figure. Someone who would teach her to cast a rod and ride a bike and put a bandage on a scraped knee when she slid too hard into first base. Celina's biological father left when he decided a child was going to get in the way of his television career. And while Angela tried to be everything to her little girl, she knew there were limits to how much she could do in any given day.

Since Celina's arrival, Angela hadn't dated, and there weren't any other people who were true caregivers for her daughter outside of a few close family members. No one filled the shoes left by Celina's absentee father, but Angela had never pushed it.

Still processing her thoughts, Angela left her purse on the table, taking only the set of keys so she could lock the front door behind her. As she set out down the street to join her daughter and Pete in this new, unspoiled moment, Angela heard the echo of her footsteps over and over. But as she got closer and closer to the picnic table at the bend in the road, the little voice in her head began to drown out the grind of her shoes on the concrete.

And with every passing step, the still small voice asked Angela if she'd been wrong in keeping Celina's primary relationships inside a small circle of trusted old friends and family. Whom had she been trying to protect more—Celina or herself?

After the sun had set in the sky, Pete and Angela followed behind Celina as she skipped back toward the house. Once they were back at the house, Angela scooted her daughter toward the door to the studio apartment and told her to take a quick shower and get her pajamas on. Celina scampered off with a smile on her face and a skip in her step— but not before she ran with open arms to Pete and gave him a bear hug-style exuberant embrace.

"Whoo-wee." Pete dragged each letter out as long as he could. "You smell like a crab net. Go get a shower, kiddo."

"Can we go again, Pete?" Her smile lit the space under the beach house brighter than a thousand fireflies.

"Well, not right now. You stink. You'd scare all the fish off."

"Fish don't have noses, Pete," Celina said, matter-of-factly.

He shook his head. "I don't think it would matter. There isn't a living creature out there who wouldn't know you were coming. Scoot, kiddo. We can go again someday soon. As long as you and your mom stay here in the apartment, the fishing spot is always right at the end of the street. It's not going anywhere."

He gave her a playful push on the shoulder. And surprisingly, the little girl ducked inside the apartment with nothing more than a nod of agreement and a big thumbs up.

Angela watched the whole exchange and the fear she'd felt creep in earlier—that she hadn't done enough, been enough for her daughter— faded away. A warmth like the perfect cup of coffee flooded the veins under her skin, and she noticed the liquid gratitude. She wished she could bottle it and bring it out for all those other moments she knew would come when she questioned her parenting.

"Thank you," she said simply.

Pete nodded, the yellow hue of the bug light made his hair glow like a highlighter marker she kept in her desk. "Anytime."

"No, really, I mean it."

The color in Pete's eyes shifted to something that reminded her of flint. If she hadn't been trying to be deliberate in expressing the simple gratitude she felt inside, she'd have missed the subtle straightening of Pete's shoulders as they shifted down and back.

"I meant it too, Angela. I don't say things I don't mean." He kept his gaze locked on her face. "She's a good kid. Helping look after her has not been a burden."

It wasn't just what he said, but how he said it, that made the warmth of the gratitude in her veins tick up a few degrees and stretch all the way from a tingle over the curve of the tops of her ears all the way down to her feet.

71

"I know she is." Angela tried to focus but kept getting lost in the feeling that was pooling into her heart. "It's just been me and her for so long. Her own father doesn't even give her the time of day. He even forgot to send a Christmas present two years ago. When he does remember, he's like Disneyland Dad, trying to throw stuff at her, so he doesn't have to invest in any time with her. We hear from him once or twice a year, if that."

The glint of steel fell from Pete's eyes. "So he doesn't have anything to do with Celina at all?"

"Not really. He didn't want her. He told me before we got married that he didn't want kids, he wanted a career—he's an anchor with Channel Four up in Houston. I agreed because I thought that's what I wanted too. Then I found out I was pregnant. Everything changed for me, but for him, it didn't. He left before Celina was born."

"He just left you?"

Angela took a deep, fortifying breath before speaking. She never talked about this period of her life. Not with her mother, her sister, anyone.

She couldn't explain why she was confessing all this to Pete. Except that he cared. He cared about her; he cared about Celina. That much was clear, even if nothing else was clear about anything since the hurricane blew through her island home.

"He was offered a promotion at the station at the same time. They wanted to promote him from reporter to an anchor on their morning show. It was a huge step forward on his career path. He'd always been clear about what he wanted. I'd grown up in the shadow of a marriage that was for the sake of the kids, where one parent resented the other one. I didn't want that for my daughter." She shrugged. It seemed like the only thing to do. "So I let him go. I told him to go."

"Oh." Pete's tone conveyed an uncertainty about the whole situation. "But he never came back? For Celina?"

Angela felt the corner of her mouth twist. "Well, no. His career took off after that. Everyone in southeast Texas knows David Carbajal. I guess he just had other things to do. But I can't resent it, Pete. He was clear with me from day one, before we were even married, and I'm the one who told him to go."

"David Carbajal? Celina's father is David Carbajal?" Pete raised his eyebrows. "Wow, when you say his career took off, you weren't kidding."

The squeak of the saltwater-rusted hinges on the apartment's door broke up the trail of conversation.

"Mama? Can you come tuck me in? Brownie and I have our pajamas on. Well, Brownie just has fur. But fur means he's not naked, right, Mama?" She helpfully held the bear out for inspection.

Angela shook her head. "No, sweetie, Brownie is perfect the way he is. Just like you are. Perfect the way God made you. I'll be right in."

"Bedtime." She pointed over her shoulder at the door, while giving Pete one last glance. "Thanks again for taking her fishing today."

"Like I said—anytime." Dual creases cut vertically between Pete's eyebrows. "Hey, Angela..."

She stopped, torn between bedtime duties for a bear and his best friend, and wanting to know the rest of what Pete had to say.

"Hmm?"

"After you tuck Celina in, if you want to come sit up on the deck for a little bit, I think I'm going to get out my telescope and look at the stars. There's supposed to be a small meteor shower tonight. I've seen a few before out here. It's amazing to watch the stars falling from out here."

Angela stood still and looked right at Pete's face. She only gave herself a second, but she looked at the gray eyes that lit up at the sight of her daughter, at the brow that furrowed when she revealed how Celina's father had left them both behind, at the jaw saved from being square by a thick dusting of post-hurricane stubble. She looked lower at the hands that had treated her when her blood sugar had dropped, the hands that had carried Celina to a safe bed to sleep in and had pulled in a small, wriggling fish on her fishing line.

"Okay. Give me a few minutes. I think she'll crash pretty quickly. She's had a big day."

Angela turned and walked the few steps to the door of her

temporary home under Pete's home. And as she tugged at the doorknob, it hit her like the splash of a stormy wave.

The stars in the sky weren't the only thing falling.

~

Pete placed two bottles of water on the top of the small round table between the two Adirondack chairs on the deck. The telescope was in the corner, and all there was left to do was wait.

He tried to tell himself he was waiting on the light show in the heavens, but as he checked his watch for the third time since sitting down, he knew he was really waiting on Angela.

But waiting for what?

He lived his professional life asking questions, getting answers, and then tying it all together for a diagnosis. That's what he'd been trained to do as a doctor. But this...this was something he couldn't identify.

What he knew for sure was that he admired Angela's steadfast resolve. Whether it was taking care of her daughter or fighting for the citizens who'd elected her, she picked up every burden in her path and shouldered it seriously, but with an unmistakable dose of grace. He also knew that the last few days, spending one-on-one time with Celina had brought just as much of a smile to his face as it had to the little girl's.

And speaking of smiles, Angela hadn't cracked too many of them since they'd met, but when she did, Pete forced himself to admit that they stayed on his mind, running in a replay loop. He'd been intrigued by her since the moment he met her. He knew if Gloria considered her a friend, then Angela met a very high standard. Gloria had been through so many upheavals and tragedies in her life that she didn't trust easily. But Angela was in her inner circle, and that spoke volumes to Pete about the kind of woman she was on the inside.

A shuffling of feet up the stairs at the far edge of the deck announced Angela's presence before she reached the top.

"Wow. What an amazing view," she said as she stepped one foot onto the deck and looked up. Specks like a child's spilled container of glitter covered the sky as far as the eye could see.

"Without any light pollution, it's amazing. All of our street lights out here are pretty dim and designed to shine straight down, instead of illuminating a greater area." Pete pointed off the front and side of the deck. "And with the gulf out front and the bay at the end of the street, it makes it even darker. I love sitting out here. If I've had a long day, it's the best way I know to decompress."

"I could sit here and not move for a year and still probably not completely decompress," Angela said as she sat in the empty Adirondack chair. "I'm not even sure I know how to relax anymore."

Pete cracked open both bottles of water and offered Angela the one he'd brought for her. "I know it's been busy for you since the forecasts showed Hope coming this way. But it won't always be like this. Things will settle down."

She took a sip of the water, then screwed the lid back on and played with the bottle absently as she stared up at the sky. "Maybe for some people. They'll get order back in their lives. They'll rebuild their homes, go back to work, start to get back to normal. But that won't happen for me."

The sadness in her voice couldn't be missed.

"Why not? Of course things will get back to normal."

"I sit in meetings all day long right now. I know what we're up against. Once we get temporary housing settled, then there's just another problem to solve. Then another and another and another. How will our businesses in downtown come back to life? Will the tourists return? They drive our economy. What about Provident College and the students there? We're still assessing the damage to Provident Medical Center and the medical school. The brief I was provided yesterday gave a conservative estimate of a year to get Provident Medical back open. You're connected there, Pete. I don't have to tell you this—Provident Medical is our largest employer. We can't have the place that provides more than a third of the jobs on this island closed for a year."

She looked squarely at Pete, and he thought he could make out a sheen of liquid along the lower lids of her eyes. There was no doubt that she took her responsibility seriously.

Maybe almost too seriously. He definitely didn't want Angela to get so stressed out that she couldn't manage her blood sugar efficiently.

He shifted in his chair slightly, turning his knees so they faced hers, separated by only a few inches. Pete felt a pull akin to the tide that flowed through the surf just out on the horizon, and he acted on it, taking Angela's hand in his own.

In medical school, he'd received surgical training. He knew how to keep his hands still, to focus on the job in front of him. But the frisson of electricity that sparked between his palm and the curve at the base of Angela's thumb almost caused him to lose his train of thought.

All he remained aware of was the stars in the sky and the softness of her skin as she allowed her hand to rest in his.

She didn't pull back. He noticed that, and with that realization, he relaxed just enough to let out his breath.

"You don't have to carry the burdens of everyone on the island, Angela. If there's one thing I've learned about Port Provident in the time I've lived here, it's that this is a true community. There is always a helping hand on this island." He held her hand lightly, indulging the connection just a little longer. "I know you hear all the commentary and see all the briefs, but no one expects you to take them all on. You're leading the charge on temporary housing. Focus on that, then when you get to a good point, find another focus area."

She didn't say anything in reply.

"Come here," Pete said, gently tugging on her hand.

She stood up as he did. He let go of Angela's hand, feeling a whisper of night air come between them. Instead of falling to his side, his hand stopped halfway and settled at the curve of her lower back. He let instinct take over and told himself to simply be, not to question it.

Just as when he took her hand, she didn't flinch. Pete pointed at the sky with his other hand. "Look at those stars."

She nodded as he gestured from one side of the horizon to the other. "Mmm-hmm?"

"Well, they're all stars. They're all bright enough to bring light to a planet, like our sun does. But none of them can brighten this whole sky on their own. But when they all work together...this is what you get."

She turned toward him. "I get what you're saying. I just don't want to let anyone down. Remember what I told you about David, how that promotion was his chance to do what he had always wanted to do? I guess in some strange way, I feel like this is mine. I've always wanted to be here, to make a difference here. As bad as it is right now, we've been given an opportunity to reimagine Port Provident and do some things we've been talking about for a while because there's virtually nothing untouched, nothing that doesn't need something to be done."

"Well, what does your heart tell you to do?"

"My heart?" Angela looked up into Pete's eyes. He questioned his focus again and tried to remind himself not to lose himself in the brown, sugary swirl around her wide, dark pupils.

"When I was talking to Pastor Ruiz the other day, he quoted a verse to me. At the time, I blew it off, but since then, it's been stuck in my head."

"What was it?"

"A verse from Jeremiah. It went something like 'Seek the welfare of the city, and in its welfare, you'll find yours'. I've been thinking about it with regard to The Grace Space."

"How so?"

"Well, I guess if I do the right thing for the people who need help, even though I have plenty of other things on my plate, I'll still be taken care of."

She nodded, then shook her head. "But you're planning on leaving in just a few weeks."

"I can still get things set up and do some good in the meantime. And so can you. One step at a time."

"I don't know if I even know how to do that anymore. I'm so used to running in ten directions at once. I'm a mom, I'm a city council member, I've got responsibilities in our family business. I guess I wouldn't even know how to focus on one thing."

Angela tilted her head and looked up at the sky. Pete followed the direction of her gaze. He looked at the moon, hanging low and yellow out over the water. Then, that pull of instinct took over again as he touched his finger to Angela's chin and gently urged it back down.

"What's the welfare of the city you need to seek?" Pete looked right into her eyes. He wanted to make sure she thought this one through, that she really understood she couldn't be all things to all people, no matter how much she wanted to be. "Your heart. What's it telling you to do?"

She leaned forward, bringing her face and her body close enough that a gulf breeze wouldn't be able to flutter between them. At the tentative touch of her hand on his chest, Pete felt his fingers press automatically a little more firmly at the small of her back.

He waited, unsure of what to do. If her hand slid up to his shoulder, if she tilted her head just so, if she gave him the slightest encouragement in any one of a hundred different ways, he knew what his heart would tell him to do.

Or at least what he'd be encouraged to do by a powerful mix of adrenaline, a dash of hormones…and a shooting star overhead.

Pete caught a fleeting burst of movement out of the corner of his eye. "Did you see that?"

She shook her head and from her lips came a slightly breathless "No, what?"

"A shooting star. The meteor shower must be getting started." Pete didn't move his hand, didn't take a step. "Make a wish."

He knew what he was wishing for right now.

Angela took a deep breath in through her nose, then closed her eyes as she let it out. She smiled, and her cheeks rounded. Her brown eyelashes laid like a whisper along the curve of her skin. Pete couldn't have looked around for another careening star if he'd wanted to. Blood shot through his veins like the fastest meteor above them.

Angela wasn't the first woman he'd ever wanted to kiss, and the stars overhead were not the first ones he'd ever wished on. But together, what they combined to make him feel—that was a first.

"I can't ask what you wished for, can I?" Pete questioned.

The smile lingered on her face, and her eyes slowly opened like the dawn of the sun over the horizon. "It's like blowing out birthday candles. You can't share, or it won't come true."

"Well, we can't have that, can we?"

Pete wasn't about to share the thoughts in his head, either. He didn't understand them all himself—he certainly didn't expect Angela to, either.

And he didn't want to scare her off. She and Celina needed a good place to stay, and there weren't many options in Port Provident right now. That downstairs apartment was perfect for their needs. It had been hard enough to convince Angela to stay in the first place. He couldn't give her any reasons to leave.

"No, no we can't." She slowly slid her hand off Pete's chest and as she moved, the night breeze stirred and flowed in the new gap between them.

The moment disappeared like the trail behind a quick-moving star overhead.

"Did you wish for anything, Pete?"

He just couldn't tell her how he'd studied her eyes, her smile, and the way his heart beat a little faster when her palm laid over it. "Not really. But I probably should have wished for a smooth opening for The Grace Space."

"Two more days. You'll be there for the opening, right?"

"Absolutely. I have a feeling your generosity and hard work is going to make a real difference in the welfare of this city in the weeks to come, Pete. From the bottom of my heart, thank you for jumping in and taking a few trucks of donated goods and some women who needed a medical checkup and out of those things, creating something that I think will be amazing."

Pete turned and leaned on the rail of the deck, looking out toward where the ocean met the sand, only a few streets away. "Amazing might be too strong of a word."

"I don't think so. It's exactly what the community needs right now. A place to come together, to see to basic needs and to feel safe. That to me is amazing. Meeting the needs of the people, right where they are.

It's why I love being on City Council, even though I feel like everything's over my head right now."

"Seeking the welfare of the city, huh?" A sense of peace filled Pete's soul. He couldn't quite put his finger on it, but it felt good to know the hours he'd spent would really make a difference.

Maybe he had dismissed Pastor Ruiz's verse and observations too easily the other day.

Maybe Pete wasn't as numb as he'd thought.

6

*A*ngela had to squint to keep the sun out of her eyes. She was actually holding her sunglasses in her hand, but Jennifer Parker was a very direct reporter, and if Angela put her shades on, Jennifer's next line of questioning would probably be to ask what Angela had to hide.

And that answer was definitely nothing. In just a few minutes, her nephew Marco—pastor of *La Iglesia de la Luz del Mundo*—would join her, Pete, and Mayor Blankenship to cut the ribbon on The Grace Space. She'd been very excited when Jennifer Parker had been able to take a break from some of her other reporting duties to come and cover this event for the *Port Provident Herald*. The more people that knew about The Grace Space, the more people that could be helped by the resources provided here.

"So, how does The Grace Space integrate into everything that's being sent to the island from other national non-profits," Jennifer asked, flipping her record button on her cell phone to capture Angela's answer.

"Well, Jennifer, this is a completely local initiative. It's separate from things that those larger, national names are here doing. We're grateful for everyone's contribution to the support and recovery of Port

Provident from Hurricane Hope. But The Grace Space is unique. It gives us an opportunity to distribute household goods and food that have been donated to area churches like *La Iglesia* from concerned groups all across the state. Plus, with the opening of the clinic area, we're utilizing the human capital we have with our world-class medical center and medical school. There are students and residents, nurses and doctors who are in limbo with the current closure of Provident Medical, and this gives them the opportunity to use their unique skills to serve the community while the leadership at Provident Medical charts a plan to reopening. Finally, we've tapped into more community resources with social services workers and lawyers to staff a Q&A area where our citizens can come and ask questions and get answers as they navigate the paperwork and such that comes with the recovery process."

"But why is this being run by *La Iglesia*, instead of being coordinated by a national organization or a government agency?" Jennifer moved the microphone end of her phone a little closer to Angela.

"Well, because everyone has a role to play in Port Provident's recovery." Angela searched for a better way to explain it than just a typical politician's sound bite. "When you look at the stars, none of them individually illuminate the night sky. But when they all work together to shine in their individual areas, the effect is a wonderful thing. This project is like that. We're all just trying to brighten the areas where we can best serve."

As she said the words, Angela's mind rewound forty-eight hours to when she stood on Pete's deck under a thousand shooting stars. She'd replayed everything about that hour in her mind a hundred times. His words made total sense as she gave more thought to them. She couldn't do everything, but with some focus, she'd be able to make what she could do the best and most effective it could be. That wasn't not serving her constituents. It was best-serving her constituents by ensuring that what she did bring to them was a full effort, not a halfway job.

What made less sense to her was the jumble of feelings that

thinking about Pete—not his words, just Pete himself—elicited in her when her thoughts strayed back to the deck and the stars and the feel of her hand in his and his hand on her waist, keeping her close.

"Angela?" Jennifer looked straight at her, with a stern look on her face. "Any updates?"

Great. She'd been caught. She could focus on one project at a time. But that project could not be Dr. Pete Shipley. The island needed her to do her best work for them. Not to fantasize about her new landlord and his gunmetal gray eyes.

"I'm sorry, Jennifer. What was that again?"

"The temporary housing. Do we have any updates on that?"

Good. She knew exactly where she stood on this subject. No confusion. No shooting stars. "We've made great progress. I hope that we will be able to make an announcement to the citizens of Port Provident by the end of this week. With ninety percent of homes in the city limits receiving some kind of damage, there is nothing that means more to me than getting our citizens out of shelters and hotels and into more stable housing situations where they can focus less on day-to-day survival and begin to move forward and recover."

Jennifer punched the red button on the screen of her phone. "Thanks, Angela. Cara Perkins came with me today, too. I think she's inside the building getting some photos. We'll run this tomorrow."

"Great. Do you have any plans to put it on the wire? I'd love to see Houston and even Dallas or Austin pick up the story and see that we're grateful for the help and that we're moving forward."

"Sure. We've been putting everything we write that's hurricane-related out there. There's a lot on the wire these days, so I don't know if you'll see this particular story picked up, but it's worth a shot."

Angela nodded. "All we can do is keep trying to spread the word. There are still good stories to tell here. It's not all doom and gloom."

Jennifer walked off to interview some of the attendees from the community, and Angela decided it was time to make her way to the front door of the sanctuary of *La Iglesia*, which had been transformed into The Grace Space for the time being. It would remain that way until the church got the insurance paperwork straightened out and had the money to begin replacing furniture and equipment and rebuilding— or until The Grace Space outlasted donations and the community's need.

A hand-painted sandwich board-style sign stood next to the door and read "Welcome to The Grace Space" in bright red letters, trimmed with a stripe of bold black around each individual letter. Someone had moved a few potted plants near the sign, as well—Angela had no idea where they'd found them—but the whole effect was cheery, and it made her smile.

Hopefully, it would bring a smile to the faces of those who needed what The Grace Space had to offer.

She walked through the door and stopped. The door swung shut and tapped her in the back. And still, she didn't move.

More hand-painted signs had been hung from the ceiling, declaring what types of items could be found where: kitchen, bedroom, toys, clothes, food. To the right, curtains had been erected to separate the small clinic from the rest of the space. The pews and tables that had once been inside of *La Iglesia* were no longer able to be used for adequate seating for church members, but they had enough usefulness left in them to make displays for all the goods that had been donated.

The Grace Space looked better than Angela could have ever dreamed. It looked almost like a real store, with aisles and departments. Pete and his volunteers had created a space where people would not be embarrassed to shop—where they could feel like they were getting a hand up, not a hand out, and could feel the care and concern from those who had donated the goods and the time to help the residents of Port Provident rebuild their homes and their lives.

She felt a flash of grateful tears well up and a lump in her throat.

And then Angela looked to the left again, and her very breath was snatched from her lungs.

Dr. Pete Shipley leaned against a pole, dressed in a white coat and scrubs. He looked completely relaxed, but completely in charge. She'd never seen him dressed like a doctor before. But if she wasn't careful, she'd get caught staring.

As she mentally chastised herself to do something—anything—but think of shooting stars and cornflower-blue scrubs, Pete noticed her, gave a wave, and took off in her direction at a quick jog.

"So? What do you think?"

The eager tone in his voice reminded her of Celina at Christmastime. All hope, all anticipation, all joy.

"It looks amazing. I was taking it all in. I can't believe how you've taken truckloads of random goods and some saltwater-soaked church furniture and turned it into this."

Pete quickly cocked one shoulder in a half-shrug. "Well, I can't take all the credit. Some amazing folks from the church and the hospital have worked right alongside me."

To underscore his point, four or five people milled around the aisles, straightening and making last minute touch-ups.

"So, are we ready to go cut a ribbon?" Pete gestured toward the door with one hand and touched his hand again to the small of her back with the other, gently guiding her.

Angela nodded, then looked up at the ceiling. She could have sworn she saw a shooting star in the church. It seemed so real that she was almost tempted to make another wish. Instead, she decided a simple prayer would do...but would God understand why she was praying about Pete Shipley and not the former pews full of donated merchandise?

The day had been long, but everything had been worth it. The Grace Space opened to many grateful hands, the clinic saw twenty-two patients needing basic wellness checks, and the mayor had expressed her thanks to Pete and the team for seeing a need and pulling together a solution so quickly. All in all, the knowledge that today had done real, tangible good for Port Provident tugged at his heart.

The jangle of a bell signaled the opening of the front door, which was strange because Pete was sure he'd locked it up more than half an hour ago when the last volunteer left. The only reason he was still inside was because he was trying to give himself a little more time to process the memories of the day and finish his notes from the clinic cases.

"The Grace Space will reopen at nine o'clock tomorrow morning." Pete turned in the metal chair at the back of the room where he'd been transcribing his notes.

A petite tornado with dark brown hair rushed across the concrete floor. He could barely believe his eyes. He'd seen Angela smile, comfort her daughter, and even share a laugh or two with friends, but he hadn't seen this kind of enthusiasm since that first quick hug in his living room the night they first talked about the temporary housing situation issues and the first steps toward creating The Grace Space.

Pete stood up, took three steps in her direction, and then was tackled by the force of her momentum colliding into him.

Instantly, he felt the spark. Whatever electricity she brought with her was transferring to him.

And he wanted more.

His arms reflexively wrapped around her shoulders, and he knew it was more about keeping her close than steadying her after the bounce after her body crashed into his.

"We did it!" Her voice came out as a shout, and she threw her head back. The silk of her hair brushed his hands where they cupped the curve of her shoulder blades.

"Did what?"

"Everything is signed for the RV park. The first trailers will be moving in tomorrow. People can leave the shelters. They can have a place to call their own while they rebuild." She gave a short jump. "Pete, you did it. Without your phone call to your friends, without making that connection, we wouldn't have been able to pull this off so quickly. We were out of options. I don't know what we would have done."

She bounced again, and this time, Pete had ducked his head to look down at her. At the first feather-light touch of her lips on his, Pete felt the full shock of the electricity Angela had brought in the room with her.

He'd wanted more, and he'd gotten it.

And he wasn't going to give it up.

Pete pulled his forearms in a little more, pressing Angela closer to him, signaling without a word that their collision was no accident. Instead of pulling back as he'd half-expected her to, she tilted her head and deepened the moment.

Losing himself in the whisper of her hair over his fingers and the hush of her breath as it mixed with his own, he forgot everything until he remembered one thing.

His last kiss with Anna.

At the shock of the memory, his fingers went limp and fell from Angela's shoulders. She pulled back as the bond of contact was lost.

"I didn't mean for that to happen," Angela said.

Pete bit the inside of his lip as he listened to her apologize. She might not have intended it, but he had. When he'd felt that first spark as she fell against him, he'd wanted to know what it was like to kiss her. He'd been thinking about it since she placed her hand on his chest on the deck when they talked underneath a sky of blazing stars.

"No, really, it's okay." He didn't know what to say beyond that. He didn't want her to feel like she'd made a mistake, but there was no way he could tell her that the memory of the woman that cancer had snatched from him caused him to back away.

He didn't want to cause awkward second-guessing—she still lived in his studio apartment, and there was no question they would run into each other. They still had The Grace Space project. And there was the connection on the temporary housing location as well. Everything needed to stay just as it was.

Speaking of all that, another question popped into his mind. "Are you going to move to the temporary housing space now?"

He wasn't sure he really wanted to know the answer, but he was grateful for the distraction from the thoughts of Anna.

"I think so. I have a group of constituents who are on the list for the first round of trailers, so that will put me back in a location where I'm accessible to them." She shifted her weight slightly onto her left foot. "Celina and I are very grateful for your hospitality in the little apartment, but it is way out there on the east end of the island. I should probably be closer in town, closer to my district."

Pete nodded. "Oh, absolutely."

He didn't feel absolute about anything right now. Five minutes ago, he'd been on top of the world with the success of The Grace Space's first day. Now, he was struggling with memories of the past and feelings he couldn't name about the immediate future.

"There's a community dinner tomorrow night at *Huarache's*—you know, Gloria's parents' restaurant. You're practically a resident of the *La Misión* neighborhood, now that you've spent so much time here at *La Iglesia* and have opened The Grace Space. You should come. I know a lot of people appreciate what you've done here and would like to thank you."

He felt a tickle at the top curve of his ears and hoped they weren't turning red. "No thanks necessary. I did what anyone would do."

"No you didn't, Pete. You did exactly what *you* would do. You had the time, but you also had the contacts to pull this off. And you have a heart for community-centered work, or you wouldn't be counting down the days until that medical mission sends you off to some corner of the world. No one else could have pulled this off like you did, in the amount of time it took you to do it." She raised an arm, hesitated slightly, then patted his forearm. "Marco says that you're *La Iglesia*'s Esther. You were sent here specifically 'for such a time as this'."

He didn't know about that. He remembered Esther from Sunday School lessons as a kid. She saved a nation. He'd organized donated cookware and checked some blood pressure. He'd done what anyone would have done in the same situation.

Wouldn't they have?

One thing he did know was the room grew uncomfortably quiet after Angela slipped out the door. The gentle whirr of a donated window air conditioning unit was the only thing between him and a lot of thoughts he'd rather not think.

It was time to go home. Past time. Of course, home was now where Angela lived right under where he walked. At least for now.

He ducked back through the curtains that made the door to the clinic space to retrieve the bags he'd brought with him this morning. When he walked back out into the main sanctuary area that now made up the store, Pete saw he was not alone.

"*Buen trabajo* today, Pedro. Really good job. When I asked for your help in bringing some order to all these donations, I never would have envisioned this. It's just incredible—just what our community needs." Marco looked squarely at Pete, scanning his face. "But you're not happy. You're troubled. Did something not go how you'd planned today?"

What a loaded question.

But there was no way he could answer Marco truthfully. They'd gotten to know each other while setting up The Grace Space and Pete felt comfortable in the pastor's presence. He was just a genuinely good guy—he saw the best in everything and everyone.

But Angela was his aunt—even though she was actually younger than Marco. You couldn't just tell a guy you kissed his aunt and started thinking about your fiancée who died.

That would be the conversational equivalent of watching a patient flatline.

He decided it would be in everyone's best interest to wave it off, to deflect.

"Long day, Marco. One of those days that was all over the map." That was accurate. *All over the map* was certainly the best way Pete could describe the thoughts in his head right now.

Marco crossed the room and sat down on one of the chairs close to Pete. "All the days lately have been long, Pedro. But that's not what I see in your eyes. Something's bothering you."

"You should consider medical school, Marco. You've got a bedside manner that could get all sorts of information out of patients."

The pastor rested his elbows on his knees. "It's a useful skill for pastors too. I guess you could call it pew-side manner."

That made Pete chuckle. "That's probably very true. But what do you do when you just can't explain something? For most of what I do, there are answers. Especially the last few years while I've been managing the birthing center. We don't have high-risk patients—we make sure that they are under the care of obstetricians who manage their care through the hospital model. In my whole time there, we've had a handful of non-emergency transfers, like when a mother has decided she'd rather get an epidural or she's been in labor for too long and isn't progressing and needs a drug like Pitocin, which requires the monitoring capabilities of a hospital. But mostly, I've found that the human body knows how to give birth. It's an instinctive, biological process."

"But whatever's on your mind isn't a textbook case, Pedro?"

Pete lowered himself into the closest chair and faced Marco. Maybe he could talk to him after all. If he just kept it vague, perhaps he could get it off his chest and go home without fear of running into Angela as he walked up the stairs to his part of the house.

Yeah, he'd keep it vague. He didn't have to bring Marco's aunt into it at all.

"Something from my past has come up, and I wasn't expecting it." Pete sat on the edge of his chair. He couldn't get comfortable, in spite of his resolve to not give too many details.

"The past is powerful, Pedro. A lot of people will tell you to leave it there—ignore it, put it in a box. Move on." His hands moved in a sweeping motion, illustrating the point. "But I don't think that is what we're meant to do."

Pete looked down. He noticed his feet. Since Anna died, his unofficial motto had been to keep putting one foot in front of the other. Keep moving. Keep going. It gave his mind a fairly regular stream of new experiences and actions to focus on.

"Moving on is all I know, Pastor. "

"But you've got to be moving *to* something, not just *from* something. Otherwise, you're running a marathon with no plan. You'll never reach the end, *hermano*." The window unit rattled to life again and gave a punctuating squeal. "So, what are you running from?"

"Anna." Her name fell off his lips with a thud. He'd thought about her, but he hadn't actually spoken of her in years. To say her name again sounded unfamiliar and clumsy. "My fiancée. She died of cancer."

Pete closed his eyes and leaned his head back. That answer was anything but vague. But he was tired. Tired of running. Tired of fearing the memory of the woman he had once loved.

"First, you're not alone. Losing someone we love means losing the vision of the future we'd planned with them." He reached out and patted Pete on the knee with a simple, reassuring touch. "But in Second Corinthians, we're reminded that when the old things pass away, Christ makes all things new. God doesn't just leave you with the old, with the memories. When I counsel people in situations like yours, I remind them that love is a gift. That person taught you how to love, how to feel. And in Heaven, they are experiencing eternal love. Love here on earth is an imperfect replica of God's love in Heaven, but now that your Anna has experienced the fullness of love in Heaven, do you think she would want you to live without any love here?"

Like a grub coming from underground to be exposed to the harsh light of the sun, Pete was taken aback. He squinted.

"But what happens to what we shared? I asked her to marry me. I was ready to take the vows, to say I was going to love her forever."

Marco raised one hand. "That's not what the vows say, Pedro. I've performed a wedding or two. The vows say 'in sickness and in health, until death do us part.' You loved her through the sickness, and then death parted you. But *hermano*, even when a log burns in your fireplace, the evidence of it is still there in the form of ashes. Love can't be erased, only transformed. If you love someone else, it doesn't wipe away your love for Anna. It changes it and makes it into something else. It never goes away because she's the one who taught you that you could love someone through anything—sickness, health, even death."

"Love never fails," Pete said, barely above a mumbled whisper.

"So you do know what Paul says about it." Marco came to his feet. "He's not wrong. We're at a time, Pedro, where we will see this whole island transformed by the rebuilding that will come our way after Hurricane Hope. But we'll still be Port Provident. The same will be true when you come to the point in your life where you're going to reconstruct that future you once saw for yourself."

Pete stood, and this time he noticed his eyes were wide open. He didn't flinch as he digested the pastor's words. "It's like the first law of thermodynamics. We can't destroy energy, only change it."

"We are told that when it's all said and done, only three will remain, *mi hermano*: faith, hope, and love. But the greatest is always love. Love may change, but it always remains."

Huarache's Restaurant, the legendary Gulfview Boulevard Mexican restaurant owned by Carlos and Juanita Garcia, was a sight for many sore eyes in Port Provident. Angela had to park almost three blocks from the restaurant. As she and Celina got closer, Angela could hear the strum of a guitar and the brassy toot of a trumpet. They'd found a mariachi band. Now she knew this was definitely a celebration everyone could enjoy. Good food, good music, good friends.

Hopefully, this would be a night to lift Port Provident's spirits.

She knew her own needed a little lifting as well. As excited as she was to see the first trailer for the temporary housing neighborhood come over the causeway to be installed at the RV park, and as warm as the community's reception to The Grace Space had been, a tug of regret had not left her heart since she walked out the door of The Grace Space after that kiss with Pete.

She hadn't seen him since then. Not at the house, in town, or at The Grace Space. And she couldn't shake the feeling that he was avoiding her. She hadn't kissed another man since David walked out of her life before Celina was born, and judging by Pete's can't-get-away-fast-enough reaction, it needed to be a long time before she kissed anyone again.

Like forever.

She kicked a rock from the middle of the sidewalk, channeling her frustration. This was why she stayed focused. This was why she didn't get distracted by emotions. This was why she put her trust only in herself, her daughter and her God.

Other people would just let her down when she was least expecting it.

She hadn't expected much from kissing Pete. It had been a completely spontaneous, unplanned reaction to her happiness at seeing so many pieces of the puzzle fall into place that afternoon. But she certainly hadn't expected him to pull back like he'd been given a glass of bitter medicine to drink.

The only bitter one here was her, though. Angela definitely felt bitterness over giving in to her impulse. Lesson learned.

The sound of the festive band grew louder with every step she and Celina took. She needed to shake out all these thoughts from her head. Tonight was a celebration for her friends and neighbors, a party thrown by two pillars of their community to come together in a spirit of survival, gratitude, and moving forward.

And with that in mind, she *was* going to move forward and put behind her that momentary lapse of judgment and all the questions and self-inflicted embarrassment caused by thinking about it again and again and again.

"Do I smell fajitas, Mama? I'm hungry! Let's go faster!"

Angela definitely couldn't argue with her enthusiasm and tugged at Celina's hand. The two of them took off in an awkward sprint, and it didn't take long for her daughter to pull ahead and drag Angela along behind.

As of right now, the only thing she was leaving behind was her encounter with Pete yesterday and all the questions that had popped up in her mind since.

"*Querida!*" Juanita Garcia stood at the open front door with outstretched arms, and as usual, a term of endearment for everyone who walked up. She knelt down to Celina's level and planted a big kiss on the little girl's cheek. "*Que bella!* And who is this?"

"Brownie the Bear. Pete let me take him home from The Grace Space." Celina proudly showed off her new furry friend.

"*Ah, mucho gusto, Cafecito el Oso,*" Juanita expressed her pleasure at meeting Brownie. "Oh, I'd heard about the great job Dr. Shipley did at transforming *La Iglesia*. Is he coming tonight?"

Since Hurricane Hope came ashore, not having all the answers had become pretty much standard operating procedure for Angela. But this one...she knew the answer to this question. "No, he's not."

"Oh, well, too bad." Juanita waved Angela and Celina inside. "The food is in the corner, the band is on the patio. Help yourself and have a good time. Tonight is a night for smiles. We've made it through the worst. Good days are ahead."

Immediately, Celina noticed a group of her friends from church and asked if she could introduce Brownie the Bear to them. Angela agreed as long as Celina stayed near her aunt Emmy, who was close to the gathering of girls. As her daughter walked toward them, Angela took a few steps in the other and headed toward the porch.

There was a coolness riding on the gulf breeze tonight, a welcome relief from the higher-than-normal humidity that had filled their air in the wake of Hurricane Hope. The mariachi band played *Cielito Lindo*, one of Angela's favorite Mexican folk songs, and she found herself humming along with the song's *ay yi yi* refrain.

"*'Canto y no llores'*—that means 'sing and don't cry,' right?" An unmistakable voice came from over her left shoulder.

So much for leaving the things she'd rather forget behind. The living, breathing embodiment of them was standing right behind her.

"It does." Angela didn't know what else to do besides to answer his question with as little extra explanation as possible.

"Then why do you look so sad? Your shoulders are slumped, and you're staring out at the waves."

Angela turned around with a small push of emotion that came out as a sarcastic laugh. "Well, because I'm still trying to figure out why I can't shake the feeling that you're avoiding me."

Pete sandwiched in next to her along the porch rail. "I was."

"Okay." Just when she thought the whole mess couldn't get any more awkward, Angela realized it could.

"But I was wrong. Will you accept my apology?" Pete turned his head toward her.

"Can you tell me why, though?" She knew she needed to accept the apology, but she also knew she had no interest in setting herself up to get burned again.

Pete paused for a moment. "I can. But that's a story best told over a plate of *Huarache's* fajitas. Can we get a plate and then talk?"

Angela turned away from the soothing roll of the waves. "Sure. Most things are better with Carlos Garcia's fajitas."

"That's the truth. After you." Pete stretched out an arm toward the dining room, and Angela slipped through the crowd and to the buffet line set up near the kitchen. She made a plate for herself and one for Celina, then brought her daughter's over to the table in the corner where the little girl sat, talking animatedly with two friends and some of her cousins.

"Do you want to go sit back out on the patio?" Pete gestured toward the far door as he held a bottle of Mexican soda. "It seems less crowded out there."

"Less crowded, yes, but far more musical. The band is still out there. I'm not sure I'll be able to hear you over *La Cucaracha*," she said as the band began to play the spirited tune.

"You're probably right. Okay, come with me." Pete began to weave through the crowd. Angela followed in his wake, pausing every few steps to return a wave or acknowledge a greeting from a friend or constituent.

Pete waited at the main door for Angela to catch up, then led the way out to the parking lot.

"Where are we going, Pete?" Angela looked around. Some folks had spilled out to the sidewalk and the curb to eat since the restaurant was near capacity, but Pete had already walked far past the last outlier.

"Right here." He stopped in front of the last vehicle parked in the lot, placed his plate and drink inside the bed of the truck, then dropped the tailgate on his dusty black pickup truck. "A tailgate tabletop. You can still hear the music, and we're not too far from Celina and your sister, but it's a little more private this way."

Private. She'd asked him for the reason why he'd kept out of her way since their impromptu kiss, but now her stomach did a small flip as she wondered what exactly the story would be, for them to need to come away from the rest of the crowd.

She set her plate in the middle of the tailgate and balanced a Styrofoam cup full of iced tea beside it, then turned around and boosted herself up.

"If I'd known there was going to be tailgating involved tonight, I probably would have re-thought wearing this sundress."

Pete settled on the tailgate with a practiced ease, and then she felt the weight of his gaze as he looked over her cotton dress, from the lace-trimmed hem that brushed her ankles to the smocked-style top embroidered with a blue flowered design.

"No, I'd say the sundress was a great choice."

His words were said in earnest, and Angela felt her stomach tingle as it did a small flip again. She gave a slight inward smile at the thought of Pete appreciating how she looked, but at the same time, it didn't match up with his most recent actions.

Now was as good a time as any to follow up on that, she supposed. She pretended she was back at a City Council meeting, asking questions about the issues at hand—it made it easier to dive right in.

"So you said you were wrong earlier and that you'd tell me why. I admit I'm curious."

Pete finished the swallow he'd just taken of his Mexican cola, then sat the curvy glass bottle with the pale green tint back down near his plate.

"Well, for starters, thanks for accepting my apology. The answer is that my reaction yesterday had nothing to do with you, although I know that sounds like I'm giving you a line." He paused and turned slightly, so he looked across the street at the edge of the Gulf of Mexico lapping at the shore.

"When I came to Port Provident a few years ago, I came here looking for a fresh start after the death of my fiancée, Anna. She had cancer and died three months after the diagnosis. It tore me up. And I've never even given a woman a second glance or a second thought since then, until I got to know you."

Angela's stomach stopped doing flips. She didn't know what kind of confession she'd been expecting, but this bombshell was not it.

Pete kept his eyes locked toward the waves. "I can't lie, I think you're an amazing person, an amazing mom, and an amazing fighter for this island. And I know what happened was a case of excitement and emotion coming together—but I guess that's what most kisses start out like. I haven't even looked at another woman since Anna died, much less kissed one, for any reason. And my reaction surprised me."

"Your reaction?" Angela found it intriguing that he was just as surprised as she'd been by his complete shut down in the middle of The Grace Space.

"I didn't want to let you go," he said simply. "And I felt disloyal to Anna's memory."

"Oh." Angela couldn't think of anything more eloquent to say. All of her skilled questioning and speaking skills that she used up on the dais at Port Provident City Council meetings had been rendered completely useless by Pete's honest confession. "I understand."

Pete looked toward Angela but didn't turn his body in her direction. "I didn't, and that was the problem. It wasn't you. It was me."

She'd said she understood, but the more she thought about it, the less she knew what to say.

"I'm probably making a mess of this, but what I'm trying to say, Angela is that I don't want to avoid you. I consider you a friend now, probably more than that if I'm being honest. And even though I didn't do a good job of showing it, I care about you. I care about Celina." His shoulders lost the iron-straight posture they'd been holding, and he shifted on the tailgate to finally face Angela. "And maybe you might let me have a do-over one of these days, if the time and place were right."

When he placed his hand tentatively on hers, she glanced in the sky to see if there were any more shooting stars.

Angela let out the breath she didn't even know she'd been holding. Since they'd met, she'd certainly come to care about Pete, to value his opinion—and she knew that's why his reaction hurt so much. She'd had more than a few bumps in the road of her life, but in the end, they'd all worked out for the best. Perhaps this was another one of those bumps. Perhaps this was one time where she needed to quit being a City Councilwoman, full of questions and research and plans, and to just let herself be a woman.

"If the time and place is right," she said with a smile.

---

7

*A*bout ten days later, on a Monday, Angela's day started early with a call from the mayor. She asked Pete if Celina could work at The Grace Space with him for the morning and rushed to City Hall.

With normal government business suspended, the parking lot was empty, and the usual hustle and bustle around City Hall was non-existent, except for Jennifer Parker, who sat on the top step of the stairs leading to the front door.

"Councilwoman Ruiz, do you have any comment about today's changes?" The reporter tapped the red button on her phone to record any answer from Angela.

Changes? What changes? Linda Blankenship hadn't given her any details, just asked her to come to her City Hall office ASAP. What was going on? And how did Jennifer Parker know before she did?

"No, no comment right now," Angela bluffed as she pushed the heavy brass-and-glass front door open and took an immediate right turn to walk up the three flights of stairs to the mayor's office, since the building's elevator needed repair.

The door to Mayor Blankenship's office stood a few inches ajar. Angela knocked and waited.

"Angela? Is that you? Come on in."

Half-filled brown cardboard boxes were placed around the room, and the bookshelves that lined the back wall had been emptied.

"What's all this, Linda?" Angela pointed at the blank shelves opposite her.

The gray-haired woman leaned back in her executive-style chair. "Change."

"I see that. Are we going to all have to move out of here so they can repair the building?"

The mayor shook her head. "No, you're not moving. I am."

Angela couldn't make heads or tails of what Linda was getting at. She needed more details. "Where? I'm really confused."

"Dallas. You know that my husband Bob is the regional vice president for American and Coastal Property and Casualty insurance company?"

Angela nodded.

"Well, last night the board of directors informed him that they're dropping the 'coastal' part. They're closing up the Port Provident office and letting most of the people go. They have a new position for him, but it requires an immediate relocation to their offices in Dallas. We talked about it last night, and with Bob's health being what it is, I'm just not comfortable being five or six hours away from him indefinitely while we repair here."

Angela felt her eyes get wide as she took in the meaning of the mayor's words.

"So, an hour ago—right before I called you—I tendered my resignation to the city manager. And according to the city's by-laws, because you're Mayor Pro-Tem until a special election can be called, Angela Ruiz, you are the new mayor of Port Provident."

Angela was taken aback. "Of all the scenarios that went through my mind when you called me this morning, I have to say this is not one I considered."

Her heart raced a bit at what now lay on the horizon for her. She wouldn't just be a key player in Port Provident's recovery. She'd be leading it.

She first ran as a candidate for City Council because she wanted to give a voice to the ideas and needs of the people she lived among and had grown up with. Their previous two representatives had been allied with developers who wanted to sell out parts of the district to the highest dollar and didn't care about tearing apart the character of the tight-knit community that had been a fixture in Port Provident since the Second World War.

But now, she had been gifted the opportunity to do so much more. Angela closed her eyes, taking it all in.

Please God, let me shine like the stars in the sky. Let me light the corner of the world you've brought me to.

"Oh, and one more thing," the outgoing mayor said, digging in her top desk drawer. "This should be yours now."

She held out a brass-colored key on a utilitarian aluminum circle-style key ring.

"That doesn't look like the keys to the offices here in the building. That's not the key to this office, right?" Angela reached her hand out to take the proffered key.

"No, it's not. It's the key to the trailer in Space One at the Port Provident Disaster Recovery Residential Community. It had been set aside for me to move into. I believe you're the leader of this community now. And you've fought so hard to make that place a reality in a short period of time. You and your sweet girl deserve Space One. Welcome home, Madam Mayor."

Linda Blankenship let go of the key, and it fell into Angela's hand. She felt the weight of it in her palm. She felt the weight of Port Provident on her shoulders.

She would just have to rise to the challenge. She would need to shine.

Pete closed up The Grace Space about an hour early after receiving Angela's text to bring Celina to the former RV park that now housed the trailers that the government relief agency had brought in. People would begin moving in tomorrow, and they'd staged a small ribbon cutting to mark the occasion.

Every step of progress, no matter how small, was celebrated in Port Provident these days as one more step on the road back to normal.

Pete parked his truck between two white vans from local TV affiliates in Houston. Space seemed to be at a premium—maybe this was going to be a bigger deal than he'd figured it would be. Pete held Celina's hand and weaved through the crowd.

Angela stood at the front, just to the side of a bow that had been tied on top of the large metal gate. A sign with the official seal of Port Provident was balanced on top of a low fence next to another sign bearing several logos from government agencies. TV cameras made a semi-circle around Angela and Mayor Blankenship, and reporters pressed in.

"This is a big day for Mommy," Pete leaned down and whispered in Celina's ear. "She's worked hard to make sure that the people who lost their homes have a safe place to stay while they're rebuilding."

"Just like we have our place with you, right, Pete?" Celina smiled.

"Exactly. Here, I'll pick you up and put you on my shoulders so you can see what's going on." He hoisted the little girl up, and she tucked her feet under his arms for greater stability. Pete's heart melted a little like butter that had been left out on the beach. Celina was so sweet and trusting, and she saw the world through a child's eyes—all wonder and newness.

The time he'd spent with her had forced him to slow down and see his corner of the world from a different angle too, like going out of his comfort zone and creating The Grace Space from the ground up.

He thought about how natural it felt to have Celina balanced on his shoulders, like he'd always been a part of her life.

Like the dad with the white picket fence he'd once hoped to become.

And then he thought about the man who could have had that chance and instead walked away before this little girl had even entered the world. As the words crossed his mind, a well-groomed man in a polo shirt and dark khaki dress pants crossed through Pete's line of vision.

David Carbajal. Lead anchor for KHOX-TV.

And Celina's biological father.

Pete's mind scrambled. What was he doing here? Anchors didn't go out to the field to do their own reporting unless something major was happening, and the ribbon cutting on a trailer park did not meet that kind of standard.

What was going on?

In spite of the afternoon heat, all Pete felt was ice. It filled every inch of his veins and poured into his stomach.

He couldn't go running up to Angela to ask what she wanted him to do—that would create a bigger scene and judging from the body language of those up front, the event was about to start.

He couldn't run away without triggering a string of six-year-old questions, which would also be disruptive to the event.

His only option was to stay put.

Pete gripped his hands around Celina's legs, where they rested on his shoulders. He would protect her. He would not let go.

And then it hit him with all the kinetic force that Hurricane Hope had brought ashore so recently. *He would not let go of Angela either.*

On the one hand, the revelation stunned him, and on the other, it fit as close and true as the pairs of latex exam gloves he wore every single day while working with patients. This wasn't about wanting to make up for a kiss that had gone awry. And it wasn't about proving that he could move past Anna's death, like he'd talked about with Marco.

It was about realizing he'd found a woman who fascinated him with her drive and her compassion and finding a family that had a spot where he wanted to belong.

"And with that, I'll turn it over to the new mayor of Port Provident, Texas, Angela Ruiz."

Pete's head snapped around as Celina let out a squeal and an extended series of excited clapping. He'd been so lost in thought that he'd missed something major. Something big enough to attract the attention of news crews and one particular newsman from Houston.

He needed to catch up on what just happened...and fast.

"Thank you, Mayor Blankenship," Angela said as she stepped to the microphone. "I know I speak for everyone in Port Provident when I thank you for your years of service to our town, and we wish you all the best in this new chapter in your life."

The crowd that had gathered behind the semi-circle of reporters applauded again. As Angela paused for the recognition of Mayor Blankenship, a ray of sun broke through one of the stray clouds in the sky. It focused its radiance just over Angela, capturing cinnamon and rust and mocha highlights mixed in with the darker coffee color. She smiled as she scanned the crowd, and it touched Pete's heart in a way he never expected.

She seemed at ease, relaxed, completely in her element. Like she'd been made for such a time as this.

"And now we are going to celebrate one more milestone as Port Provident continues the work of rebuilding from Hurricane Hope. I'm happy to announce that behind me is the Port Provident Disaster Recovery Residential Community. A lot of people have made this happen today, and I'm glad to announce that by the end of the week, we will have moved everyone out of the temporary shelter at the high school and into housing here. These aren't just trailers that people will live in for a few months while they rebuild their homes. They're bringing hope after Hurricane Hope. And that's going to be my theme as we rebuild our island—we are going to bring hope to our citizens. And as the mayor, I'll be right alongside you, living in Space One as I rebuild my own home."

The assembled crowd clapped again, and so did Celina. Angela turned and walked over to the gate that blocked the driveway. She unlatched the pin that held it shut and swung the metal barrier wide open.

"Welcome home, Port Provident," she exclaimed, loud enough to be heard without the microphone. Flashbulbs went off, capturing the moment—but the sun and the flashes were no match for Angela's high-wattage smile, demonstrating her pride in the little housing development and in the community that she now led.

As the crowd disbanded and some of the residents went to go inspect their new temporary homes, Pete tried to hang back at the edge of the grassy lawn, still unsure of what to do about David Carbajal.

While thinking about the best course of action, he noticed David wrapping up with his camera crew and unhooking his microphone. David strode over to where Angela stood, talking animatedly with two citizens.

The crowd had disbursed so Pete could hear Angela clearly as she spoke to David. "Not right now. You need to wait your turn."

The tone in Angela's voice was all business. Pete stayed where he was, bouncing up and down a bit to distract Celina into thinking he was a horse. He didn't want to bring Celina any closer, but he didn't want to leave Angela by herself, either. The best course of action seemed to be to wait and see. He was used to that. He did that all the time while attending births. Just wait and see how things progressed—usually everything worked out on its own timetable.

After the two women walked off, David asserted his place as the next in line.

"This is off the record, Angela. This isn't a reporter and the mayor. This is you and me."

Angela folded her arms across her chest. "Mmm-hmm. What do you need, David? It's been six years. It figures that you only come back to talk to me when I get the mayor's position."

"I told you, that's not what this is about."

"Then what is it?" She raised her eyebrows. Pete observed a flicker in her sugary eyes, which were quickly turning a much darker shade than he'd ever seen.

"It's about Celina. This is no place to raise a kid, Angela." He pointed straight at the white RV with a gray and blue stripe pattern down the side which had been designated as Angela's. "Plus, with your new role as mayor, you're going to have too much work to do to keep an eye on her in a place like this."

"A place like this? David, this isn't a maximum security prison. It's an RV park. And it's full of Port Provident residents. You know, like you used to be. The people here are good people." She adjusted her arms, crossing them even more tightly around her ribcage. "I've kept an eye on Celina just fine for the last six years. I don't need parenting advice from someone who isn't a parent."

He spoke with measured, newscaster tones. "I am now, Angela. I remarried three years ago. She has a five-year-old, and we have a two-year-old of our own."

Angela's arms dropped to her sides. "What are you getting at?"

"I never terminated my parental rights, Angela. She needs to be in a place where she's safe, not in some refugee camp. I'm happy to have my lawyer explain it to yours if I need to."

"Six years without an in-person visit. You even forgot Christmas, David. *Christmas*. You really think you have her best interests at heart?"

"I do," he said with no irony in his voice.

Pete saw Angela's face blanch. Standing back on the curb was not an option. He could clearly see that the time for waiting and seeing had passed. This situation needed a change, stat.

He covered the distance between them in four quick strides, keeping Celina on his shoulders. She thought it was a game. He thanked God as he walked that she had no idea what they were heading toward—or who they were heading toward.

"It's not fair of you to put Angela on the spot like that. Of course she's not going to agree to anything at the site of a press conference." Pete held on tight to Celina. He reminded himself that he would never let go. "You can come back after she's had time to think about it."

"Who's this? The babysitter?" David threw a gaze at Pete, but never changed his granite-hard expression as he took in the face of his daughter.

"Dr. Pete Shipley, Medical Director of The Grace Space."

The TV anchor extended his hand in a cursory way. Pete refused to shake it. To do so would have meant moving his hand from where it steadied Celina.

And he was never letting go.

David recognized they were at an impasse and lowered his hand. "Two days, Angela. I'll be back on Wednesday."

He turned around and walked back toward the white van with the brightly colored news station logo on the side.

"Who was that, Mama?"

Angela looked up at her daughter and looked back at the man who had given the little girl half her DNA. "Just someone I used to know, Celina. Don't worry about him."

Pete finally moved his hand from Celina's leg, but only to cup it around the curve of Angela's shoulder.

"You don't need to worry about him, either."

They dropped Celina off at the hotel room where Angela's sister Emmy was staying. Emmy had agreed to watch Celina and feed her dinner while Angela cleared her head.

What a rollercoaster of a day.

It all crashed down on her as Pete drove them back down Gulfview Boulevard. She was so thankful she was in the passenger seat because there was no way she could concentrate on anything except David's ugly threat right now.

Angela bit her lip. The last thing she needed was to let her emotions get the best of her and to start crying. But that's what she wanted to do.

She just wanted a good cry, a warm bath with some scented bath crystals, a chocolate-covered strawberry or two, and the chance to just dump out all the emotions she'd been carrying since the storm hit. She could handle the pile-on of official things, as they related to her role in city government. But an insult to her parenting and a threat to take her daughter away—that was just too much. It tipped the scales, and violently so.

Pete pulled the truck into a parking spot along the wide sidewalk that topped the seawall which defined the edge of Port Provident, right where the city met the sand and surf.

"Let's get you out of the car and into the fresh air. We're going for a walk."

"Pete, I don't really want to walk…" Angela trailed off. She didn't know what she wanted to do exactly. Well, except maybe run somewhere far away where no one would ever make threats to take her baby girl from her ever again.

"I know you don't. But I need you to trust me."

Staring blankly out the passenger side window, Angela couldn't even bring herself to look at him—at anything. Finally, she heard the driver's side door open and then shut after Pete got out of the truck. He came over to her side and popped the door. He offered his hand through the opening, then took hers and gently coaxed her out.

Locking the door behind him, they walked down the narrow staircase from the raised seawall to the beach.

"They've gotten this area pretty well cleaned up," he said. "It's amazing how much work has been done in such a short period of time."

Angela nodded, not trusting herself to speak. They walked along in silence for a few minutes. She continued to hold Pete's hand, his fingers lightly threaded through hers. The clasp was so loose that she feared a strong breeze might blow their hands apart, but in spite of the fragility, she took a great deal of strength from it.

They reached a large granite chunk that had been displaced from a grouping at the base of the seawall.

"Let's sit right here," Pete said. He helped her perch on the pink-flecked stone, then sat down beside her, taking her hand again once they were both settled.

She watched the waves roll from the horizon to the shore, all the words she wanted to say welling up inside her just like the tide.

"I've lost just about everything," she finally said in a low voice. The words pushed out of her, matching the ebb and flow of the surf. "I've lost my home. I've had everything inside of it taken away. I'm not going to let my daughter be taken away too."

Pete gave her hand a reassuring squeeze. "I know. It's not what I want for either of you."

"He hasn't laid eyes on her in six years, then he decides to show up for a press conference he wouldn't normally ever attend—just so he has an opening to get to me. He knew I wouldn't be able to get away, not with the other media and the rest of the crowd. He knew I'd be cornered."

Her shoulders shook with a chill that had nothing to do with the weather.

"Can I play devil's advocate for a minute?"

Angela wanted to tell him no, she'd already come face-to-face with a devilish scheme today and she wasn't interested in any more. But that was more of a fight than she could put up right now, so instead, she just nodded her head affirmatively.

"Don't hate me for saying this, Angela, but what if he's right? I've been thinking about it. I saw him almost immediately once Celina and I staked out our spot this afternoon. I watched him like a hawk during the press conference. When he started talking to you, I just held on to Celina, ready to take off running if I needed to in order to protect her. I'd do anything to protect her, and I hope you know that."

Angela nodded again, this time with much more conviction. She couldn't question the bond that had developed between the doctor and her daughter in the short time they'd known each other.

"So I don't get it. Why did you say he might be right? I thought you were on my side." His assertion burned, like the brush of tentacles on a jellyfish.

"I am on your side. Always. But I'm on Celina's side too."

"No," the syllable came out on a choked sniffle. "If you're for him, you're not for either one of us." Angela pulled her hand away and relocated it squarely on top of her knee.

"I don't know him, other than watching the ten o'clock newscast from time to time. I don't know if he's a good person or a bad person. Only you can be the judge of that. You did say you let him go because he'd always been upfront with you on the subject of children and his career." Pete paused but didn't make a move to reach for her hand. He looked out at the water. "Look, I'm not expressing myself well here. I don't know him. All I do know is that I lost someone I loved. I know what it's like to live with regret, wondering why you didn't say or do something when you had the chance. If he's gotten married and had a change of heart and now knows what a blessing kids are, what if this storm is the crazy opportunity for him to change his relationship with Celina? What if one of the hopeful things that comes out of Hurricane Hope is the chance for Celina to grow up without regretting that she didn't have the chance to know her father?"

He stopped abruptly, as though holding himself back from saying any more.

"No." There wasn't anything more for Angela to say than that. "He hasn't done anything to show he deserves a role in her life. Just because he has a role in some other kids' lives doesn't mean he's done anything to deserve a role in my kid's life."

Angela slid awkwardly off the rock, feeling the rasp and pull of the rough edges against the fabric of her sundress.

"I'm ready to go now. Drop me off at Emmy's hotel room. I'll just spend the night there. With my daughter."

The wet sand pulled at her shoes with every footstep, but she had no intention of slowing down. Pete needed to understand she was serious—about leaving and about how wrong he was. This whole conversation had been a waste of her time.

As she waited for the door of the truck to unlock, Angela looked down at her shoes.

She didn't dare look up at the stars.

8

On Wednesday morning, Pete didn't see Angela's car in its usual parking space under the house. He didn't hear any sounds coming from the apartment, either—which led to a suspicion he couldn't shake.

Feeling a little bit like a super spy, he raised up on his toes and gave a glance through the kitchen window. The apartment was neat as a pin. Too neat, in fact.

Brownie the Bear was gone from his perch of honor on the bed.

Pete knew it meant one thing and one thing only: Angela had moved out without saying a word. And while it bothered him, he knew he only had himself to blame. Although he knew he was playing devil's advocate while they talked on the granite rock, he didn't know he was going to upset Angela quite so deeply. He'd brought it up strictly because he knew the pain of missing someone who should have been a part of your life. He loved Celina too much to let her possibly grow up with a hole in her heart if that could be avoided.

He stopped himself and reprocessed his last thought—*he loved Celina too much...*

And then it hit him, it wasn't just Celina. He loved Angela too much to just say what she wanted to hear. He loved her too much not to speak the truth on his heart and his mind. He loved her too much to...

Wait.

He stopped himself.

The bottom line was Pete loved Angela too much.

He didn't think he could ever fall in love with another woman again, not after losing all his hopes and dreams with Anna to the beast known as cancer. But he'd been proven wrong. Love could change form, love could extend to others, love could expand and transform—but the essence of love remained, just as Marco had said. A heart that had known love once, had known the joy brought by love and the dreams inspired by love, would one day wake up and realize a thirst for love again.

Who would have known it would take the deluge of a hurricane to finally relieve his parched heart?

But now he had a problem. And he had to make it right.

He had patients waiting for him at The Grace Space, but before the day was over, everything would change. He would see to it.

Pete put his handwritten notes from Mrs. Diaz's appointment into her folder. Due to the conditions on the island, the record system at The Grace Space clinic was pretty primitive. But Pete took detailed notes on everyone he saw, filed them all in individual folders donated by a church in Austin, and would be turning them over to everyone's primary physician at Provident Medical once the doors reopened. He did what he could for now to safeguard all patient information, and as more infrastructure came back to the island, he would apply that to his recordkeeping here.

He felt good about the work he was doing. It was the most basic of medicine, but with each and every patient he saw, he knew he was making a difference—even if it was a small one. It reminded him of why he'd applied to Mercy Medical Mission in the first place.

He had expected to hear from the team at Mercy Medical Mission by now. The date that they'd given him as a follow-up had passed late last week, but he'd been so busy here at The Grace Space that Pete hadn't realized they hadn't contacted him when they said they would.

"Pete Shipley?"

His patient appointments were through for the day, so the voice behind him caught Pete off-guard.

"Yes." He stood from the table and turned around.

"I'm Jake Peoples, Executive Director of the Peoples Family Foundation here in Port Provident." Jake put out his hand, and Pete returned the gesture with a hearty shake.

"Gloria's brother-in-law, right?" If he recalled correctly, Jake Peoples had married Gloria's sister Gracie about two years ago, and they now had a young daughter. Gloria had delivered the baby, but Pete remembered seeing them around the clinic.

"Her favorite brother-in-law." The man laughed. "I'm her only brother-in-law, but as picky as she is, I'm claiming the title."

Pete gestured toward the nearby plastic chair. "She is that. Please, have a seat. How can I help you today, Jake?"

Jake sat down and rested a leather-covered portfolio in his lap. "Actually, this visit is about how I can help you."

"I don't understand," Pete said. He didn't really know Jake Peoples, except in the most six-degrees-of-separation kind of way, so he didn't know how Gloria's brother-in-law could provide any kind of assistance. "I've got the clinic well-staffed with residents and doctors from Provident Medical Center, and volunteers from the church are filling the positions in the main store area of The Grace Space."

"Right. And they're doing a great job. Your little project has gained a lot of notice both in and out of Port Provident. At the Peoples Family Foundation, our mission is to fund projects that build into the lives of the residents in Port Provident. My great-grandfather was one of the key townspeople in rebuilding Port Provident after the Great Storm of 1910. Since then, my family has tried to stay active in bringing out the best in our city. Projects like The Grace Space are a special favorite of my grandmother's, and she asked me to reach out to you."

"I'm glad to hear the work we're doing here is resonating. But I still don't quite follow where you're heading."

"The Peoples Family Foundation would like to see The Grace Space become a permanent fixture in Port Provident." Jake opened his folder and held out a few pieces of paper and one blue rectangle and handed it to Pete. "I'd like to give you that check today as a sign of our commitment to the project, plus a contract for a one-year lease on a Peoples Property Group building at Avenue K and 34th Street. It's a great historic building, a corner market that was built in 1907. The downstairs would be perfect for your store and donation center, and the upstairs residence can be easily retrofitted into a primary clinic space. We're prepared to cover the costs on that and help make the project a success. Are you interested?"

Pete looked at the check. Several zeroes were written on it—a substantial sum and a substantial endorsement of the work that had been done at The Grace Space.

"I almost don't know what to say, Jake. This is very unexpected."

"I figured it would be, but I like surprises. Gloria told us about closing the birth center. She said you were looking at some other options. My Nana really likes this project, so she asked me to offer you one more option."

Pete could feel different parts of his heart being tugged in different directions—right, left, up, down. Nothing was easy.

This was an incredible opportunity. When he started organizing that first truck of donated goods, Pete had no idea that it would become a project he had so much pride in and that it would grow so quickly. But at the same time, Mercy Medical Mission had been his dream for years.

And then there was Angela.

Of course, if she didn't accept his apology—whatever that wound up being—that would be one direction closed to him forever. And he'd have no one to blame but himself.

"When do you need an answer by, Jake?"

"How about Monday at the latest?"

He had a lot to think about, and a maximum of five days to do it in. "I can make that work."

He and Jake both stood and shook hands, and Jake left the clinic area.

Now it was time to see if he could make his apology to Angela work. Whether he stayed in Port Provident or got the call from Mercy Medical Mission and moved to some far-flung corner of the world, Pete knew he could not just leave the charged conversation on the beach as the last word between him and the woman he realized he'd come to love.

~

Angela sat at a window-side table in Porter's Seafood, waiting for David to join her for what she was certain would be the most awkward meal ever.

She did not want to talk to him. She did not want him to talk to her daughter. She did not really know why she was even here, much less early.

Waiting gave her too much time to be alone with her jumbled thoughts.

And while she couldn't make sense of most of the words floating around in her mind, over and over and over again, she heard Pete's voice, talking about the hope to be found in Hurricane Hope.

Angela didn't think Pete was right about giving David a second chance, and anyway, she was not a woman to give second chances easily. She'd been on her own for far too long, burned by too many people—David Carbajal included.

Pete Shipley was included, too, if she wanted to make the list complete. She'd never expected him to say what he said Monday night. She expected him to say David was crazy and that she needed to tell him to take a long walk off the 89th Street Pier.

But he didn't. And his stupid take on this stupid situation had kept her up for the last two nights. Even moving out from underneath Pete's house to her new RV had not allowed her to get any rest.

"Angela, thanks for meeting me." Her ex-husband pulled out the chair directly across the table from her and sat down. "I know I took you by surprise on Monday. We haven't been on good terms for years —I just wanted to get in front of you, not on the phone, not by text or email, not your assistant calling mine. I wanted to speak directly to you. I know you don't have any reason to trust me where Celina is concerned, but I need you to know I'm coming at this from the right place. There's no ulterior motive."

Angela took a long sip of her iced tea while she collected her thoughts. "If it was the hurricane you were so worried about, why didn't you call before landfall—like when the evacuation order was issued—and make sure she had a place to stay? That makes more sense than weeks later when we're about to move into our own place. If it was that you're a father now, why didn't you call when your baby was born? I just don't understand, David."

The waiter came and took their order. Angela declined an appetizer. No sense in dragging this out. She'd skip straight to dessert if she could.

"I've messed up, Angela. A lot. All your questions are valid. My only response is I could have done everything better. But I'm hopeful that you'll give me the chance to get to know my daughter and to prove that my priorities in life are different now."

Hopeful?

Angela's ears perked up at the sound of that word. Pete had been hopeful too. She was the only one without hope in this situation.

"I was selfish, Angela. I was focused on myself. I don't really deserve a second chance, but I have a family now. My perspective has changed. And I don't want to wake up one day and realize I have a great relationship with the family that's under my roof, but I don't know my daughter at all. I want to know I at least tried to change the situation. I don't want to take her away from you. I don't want to go back to court and argue custody. I just want to know my daughter—and if I can help her in this crazy time for you both, then I want to do that."

She'd heard this speech before. Monday night on a granite rock, to be exact. Was God trying to get her attention by making her hear it again?

Angela knew she couldn't just erase more than six years of hurt.

She didn't even really know how to start. But what if he was sincere? What if her own stubborn heart and her own years of hurt kept her daughter away from something that could be good in her life?

What kind of parent would she be?

She thought again of Pete, taking Celina fishing at the small pier at the end of his street. In her mind's eye, she clearly saw the joy on her daughter's face as she shared in that father-daughter type of experience.

Celina had loved the attention from Pete—the stuffed bear, someone to play dance-style video games with, someone who talked with her, made sure she was safe and well-cared for at The Grace Space, and someone who baited her hook.

Angela knew that now that David had opened the door, she couldn't just kick it shut. She still didn't know if she wanted to throw it wide open, but she had to steel the nervousness in her veins and at least have this conversation with David.

"What did you have in mind?" Her mouth felt dry as she formed the words, but as soon as she got them out, she felt a little bit of relief. They were out there.

She inserted a prayer in her mind as she waited for David's answer. *Please God, take this conversation where You want it to go. I can't decide this on my own. Make it clear to me.*

"Maybe we could just hang out." David shrugged. "There's a beach right over there. Does she like sandcastles?"

Angela relaxed a little bit. Sandcastles seemed like something small but possibly meaningful. "Yes, she does. But everything in our house was ruined in the hurricane. I'm pretty sure we don't even have a bucket or shovel to use."

The waiter placed an entrée in front of each of them. "That's okay. I bought one on my way down here. I hoped you'd say yes."

More hope.

He'd come prepared, thought ahead, thought of someone else. The David she used to know never would have done that. He was too busy chasing stories and taking care of his own needs and goals.

Angela felt a stir in her heart. Maybe she could have a little hope too. Maybe it would be enough.

After they'd finished eating, Angela called Emmy and asked her to bring Celina to the beach. Angela steadied herself and with a deep breath, introduced her daughter to her father. Angela was amazed by the generosity of her daughter's spirit.

Celina wasn't fazed by the six years of absence. She didn't ask why he left before she was born. She didn't question where the Christmas presents were the year she was four. She didn't need to know where he'd been. After the introductions, Celina just smiled, grabbed the bucket, and started digging in the wet sand by the shore.

And that was that.

They spent two hours there, building sandcastles and watching Celina splash through the ankle-deep water. Never in a million years would Angela have thought she could spend an afternoon in David's presence and enjoy it. He had taken the day off from anchoring the six o'clock news but had to be back in time to sit in the anchor's chair at ten o'clock, so as the afternoon began to roll into evening, David headed back home.

He didn't bring up anything about Celina's living arrangements again. Angela's mind began to second-guess things and start running through worst-case scenarios. He said he didn't want to take her back to his house or rehash a custody arrangement...but what if...

Angela shut the runaway train of thought down. She would not let her mind engage in these scenarios.

No. She would judge David based on his words and actions from today, not those of the past.

She would have hope.

She would hope for the best. Celina deserved that, and so did her own heart. She had been entrusted with the honor of leading Port Provident, a job that would require vision and optimism in these crazy days ahead.

Shouldn't she lead her own life in the same way?

. . .

Later that night, Angela sat on the edge of the bed next to Celina. She tucked the sheet around the little girl's shoulders and tuck-tuck-tucked all the way down to her feet.

"Snug as a bug in a rug, little one."

Celina wore a tired but pleased smile. "I had fun today, Mama."

"I could tell, Sweetie. How do you feel about everything—meeting your dad and finding out you have a half-brother and a step-sister?"

She yawned satisfyingly. "I think it's great, Mama."

"You do?" Angela wasn't sure what answer she expected, but this one still took her a little bit by surprise.

"Well sure," Celina reiterated, matter-of-factly. "You can never have too many people who care about you."

The simplicity of her daughter's assessment almost brought tears to her eyes. This had to be what the Bible meant about faith like a child. This simple trust, this face-value acceptance struck her heart, and Angela knew she'd be thinking about that one sentence for a while.

"No, *mija*," Angela said, addressing Celina with the Spanish endearment for daughter. She pressed a gentle kiss to her baby's forehead. "You certainly can't."

Pete hesitated as he turned through the gate of the RV park. He wondered if he should turn around. Maybe she just wanted to be left alone. Would he be making things worse by stopping by?

He saw Angela sitting on the step to the door of her RV. As his headlights splashed on the ground near her, she looked up.

Too late. She'd noticed him. He couldn't turn around now. Well, if she didn't want to listen to what he had to say—then he'd just turn around and leave. He would respect her wishes, if that's what it came to. That was part of love. Doing what was right for the other person, even when it was hard.

He parked the truck near her trailer and pulled out the box he'd brought with him.

"I brought a housewarming gift. I picked out some things from The

Grace Space. Thought you might could use some dishes and such for your kitchen. I didn't know if they stocked these trailers with anything to help you get started." Pete placed the box at her feet.

"I owe you an apology," she said softly.

"I owe you one, too. I shouldn't have said what I did. I spoke from the heart, but I'm not a parent. I can't really speak on those kinds of decisions." Pete continued to stand a few feet back, unsure of whether or not his presence was going to be welcome.

Angela looked past Pete. "I can hear the waves from here. It reminds me of sitting up on the deck at your house. A lot reminds me of you these days. I shouldn't have left like I did. You've been nothing but generous to me and Celina. I thought I was protecting Celina by leaving so I wouldn't run into you and have to continue our conversation from the beach. But instead, I was acting in a way I'd never let my six-year-old act."

"You had your reasons."

She laughed a little. "Well, yeah, but they were the wrong ones. You cared enough to be honest with me and to speak what was on your mind. And I was afraid of it, so I ran off."

Angela leaned over and looked inside the box Pete had placed near her feet, then continued her deliberate train of thought. "David came back to town today, like we agreed on Monday. We had lunch. I didn't really want to listen to what he had to say, like I didn't want to listen to what you had to say. Until one word caught my ear. He said he was hopeful that he could make things right. It reminded me of what you said, about the hope—the good—that could come out of Hurricane Hope. I felt like God was trying to get my attention by having you both say the same thing."

"And?" Pete wanted her to speed up the careful pace of her words. He was beginning to have a little more hope himself.

Angela exhaled noticeably. "And so I had Emmy bring Celina to the beach after lunch so she could meet David. They made sand castles."

Pete's first thought was about the little girl he'd grown to care for. "What did Celina think of it all?"

Angela looked straight at Pete for the first time since he'd walked up. Her complexion was slightly yellow, tinted by the glow of the street light overhead. "It was just another day at the office to her. She didn't ask questions. She didn't judge. She just accepted it—and David. When I asked her about it at bedtime tonight—I wanted to know how she felt about David and being told she had siblings, of a sort—she told me she thought it was a good thing because you can never have too many people who care about you."

"What a smart kid." Pete's heart warmed at hearing the little girl's wisdom.

"You know, she's right." Angela stood up from the step and took two steps forward. Pete could smell the mountain floral scent of the detergent that had washed the T-shirt she was wearing. "You can never have too many people in your life who care about you. I've been so busy for so long that I haven't had many people like that in my life. I have my family. I have my daughter. I have a handful of close friends, mostly from *La Iglesia*. But they're all the same people who have been there for years. I don't seem to cultivate new friendships easily. I've focused instead on raising my daughter and building my role at City Hall. And then a hurricane blew you into my life. And I realized there's someone in my life I truly care about. He cares about my daughter."

She took one step closer and lifted her arms, letting them come to rest around Pete's neck.

"And I hope he cares about me."

Her breath tickled his lips. Her words were exactly what he needed to hear in order to lose his heart.

"He does."

Pete had been trained to make life-and-death, split-second decisions. He relied on that instinct and let his mouth connect with hers, bringing them together with all the blaze of those shooting stars they'd watched on his deck. Then, they'd come so close—but they'd stayed apart.

Now, nothing was keeping him from the taste of her, from the scent of her, from the feel of her as he wrapped his arms around her and drew her in.

An ocean breeze picked at her hair, stirring tendrils across both his cheek and his hand. The breeze wrapped around them like a frame, giving a border to this moment in time—a moment he would never forget.

When at last they pulled away from the kiss, Pete waited to see if they would pull away from each other. They didn't—she kept her forearms resting lightly at the curve of his shoulders, and he let his hands linger at the top flare of her hips.

As he'd arrived earlier, Pete had been worried that Angela wouldn't let him stay.

Now he worried he'd never want to leave.

Angela smiled to herself as she walked up the steps to Pete's deck Friday night.

"Pete! We're here! And Brownie the Bear came too!" Celina decided to take the steps two at a time, practically sprinting up to where Pete stood next to his grill.

Pete leaned down and gave Celina a big bear hug and lifted her off the ground so she kicked her toes and squealed. He was doing all the right things, but Angela could tell something was not quite right.

"What's the matter?"

Pete looked up at her, a lopsided half-frown showing in the middle of the beard stubble.

"I still hadn't heard back from Mercy Medical Mission, so I decided to call on my way home today and follow up on my paperwork. I was connected to someone in Human Resources, and after a few minutes of conversation, she told me that they're not accepting new applications right now and they're not planning to do any new placements until early next year."

Angela sat down the bag of chips she'd brought for dinner. The grocery store on the island had just reopened yesterday, and although they weren't fully stocked yet, it felt good to do something normal, like buy a bag of salty, crunchy potato chips. Her mouth watered just thinking about opening the bag and biting into a chip.

"I thought you'd been told your application was pretty much a formality and they had a place to put you."

"That is what I was told, too. I know quite a few people there, some pretty high up in the organization. More than one person told me there was a place for me." He continued to bounce Celina, but Angela could tell his mind was bouncing too. He seemed far away from the wooden deck with the soul-calming views.

"Well, maybe it was a mistake. Maybe this person didn't really know. You work with insurance companies—surely you've talked to plenty of customer service representatives who don't have a clue what the real deal is."

He cracked a smile. "You got me there. But no, this was the head of HR. She's in charge of all the hiring. She said they're not doing any right now, period."

Celina broke in the conversation to ask if she could go inside and play her favorite dance video game. Pete agreed, and the little girl ran off at a rabbit-quick pace.

"So what are you going to do now?" Angela came up close behind him as he laid hamburger patties on the grate of the hot grill. "Maybe you could re-open the clinic?"

"No, that's a done deal. I signed paperwork yesterday to put the clinic on the market. A friend of mine who is a real estate agent knows a developer who is buying distressed properties like mine to fix up and flip. Melissa Miller thinks she can have it sold by next week."

"Oh. So you wouldn't be staying, regardless?" Angela thought of that kiss at her temporary trailer, of how he fit in Celina's life with such natural ease…and of how she'd caught herself doodling a heart in the upper corner of a briefing paper she'd been given during a meeting this morning.

She wasn't the type to doodle. And she wasn't the type to easily fall in love. In fact, she'd only done that one other time, and she'd spent the last six years telling herself she had no interest in repeating how that turned out.

Fleetingly, she wondered if an acting mayor could command a citizen to stay in town?

The very idea had too many shades of Henry VIII manipulating his court. This wouldn't be a viable option. And besides, she would feel like a complete idiot for trying to convince someone to alter their life based on one kiss. Rational people didn't do that. And she had to stay rational. While meeting Pete in the wake of the hurricane was a nice distraction, the fact of the matter was she didn't need to be distracted. She was now the mayor of Port Provident, Texas. She had almost fifty thousand people looking to her to lead and rebuild their city. They weren't looking for her profile on a dating website.

"Well, actually, there's been a development there." Pete lowered the lid on the grill and turned to face Angela.

She felt her heart do a little bounce and it surprised her. She had never been the bouncing heart type. Not until she met a doctor who cared about her daughter and her city as much as she did.

"What do you mean?" Angela couldn't contain her curiosity, but tried to hold her hope in check.

"Do you know Jake Peoples? The Peoples Family Foundation?"

Angela nodded. "They've been around for generations. I think everyone knows Jake and his family. But what does Jake have to do with you staying in Port Provident?"

"He came to visit me at The Grace Space the other day. His grandmother likes the concept of what we're doing and wants The Grace Space to become a permanent fixture in Port Provident. He handed me a check and a contract for a suitable piece of real estate if I wanted to stay and make it happen. That's why I called Mercy Medical Mission today. I have a deadline to let Jake know one way or the other."

"So you'd consider running The Grace Space full time?" She had to pull even harder to keep her hope from floating up like a balloon.

Pete gestured to the Adirondack chairs nearby and took a seat. Angela followed him.

"Well, that's where I'd like your opinion."

That bouncing heart feeling came back. All day long, Angela was asked for her opinion on things. It was part of being mayor. But coming from Pete, this request seemed to carry a whole different type of weight. She tried to not get ahead of herself—but the little flutter persisted.

"Okay, shoot." She tried to stay monosyllabic so she could sound calm.

"Well, what would you think of that? If I stayed?"

Angela knew exactly what she'd think, but she wasn't sure she was ready to reveal those thoughts to Pete yet. She hardly felt comfortable revealing them to herself.

She decided on the diplomatic, mayoral route. "I think Port Provident would be a better place if you stayed. We can use people like you here."

"Angela." His voice was firm. "I didn't ask for the mayor's opinion. I asked what you would think. I think there's something here between us. I've felt it grow and I felt it Wednesday night, and I think you do too. I want to know if I'm right. Do you want me to stay? Do you think there's anything to build between us?"

Pete's straightforward line of questioning stripped all the fluff, all the bravado out of the words she had been trying to use.

Hurricane Hope had torn through Port Provident, stripping away all the basics of the town and left those who called it home no choice but to take what was left and build and make things better.

Angela looked Pete straight in his flint-and-steel-colored eyes. Hurricane Hope had brought him into her life, too. And her feelings for the future with him were no different than the feelings she had regarding her city.

The only choice was to build.

The longer she hesitated, the more she carefully couched her words, the more time would be wasted. She only had one answer.

"Yes, Pete. It's there. It's real. There's a foundation to build on, and I'd like you to stay."

"I'm glad to hear that Angela. I hoped I'd gotten the diagnosis right." He stood up from the chair and headed for the grill. "I also hope

I get these burgers right. It's sure nice to have a grocery store open again, even if it's only half-stocked."

"I agree. Just one more baby step on Port Provident's road to recovery. There are so many pieces to the puzzle, but with each little one that fits into place, I become more confident that we're going to build back better than before. I've decided I'm definitely going to run for mayor when the special election is called. I don't want this to just be a temporary role I'm filling. This is what I want to do with my life."

Pete slid the final burger patty on a bun and closed the lid to the grill. "You know what I want to do with my life?"

His grin quickly spread from ear to ear, giving Angela butterflies at the sight of his timeless good looks.

"Run a medical clinic that the Peoples Family Foundation is backing?"

"Good one. But that wasn't what I was thinking of. I was thinking I'd like to kiss the mayor of Port Provident. Maybe more than once. Are there any laws against that, Madam Mayor?"

Never had government been so rewarding. She felt the corners of her mouth pull upwards in a smile just as playful as Pete's. She hoped he planned to make good on his life goal soon.

Like before dinner.

And maybe again afterward.

"Not that I'm aware of, Dr. Shipley. Would you like for me to consult the city code?"

He left the plate on the shelf next to the grill and came back to the chairs, then reached out his hand. She laid her fingers on top of his and never broke eye contact or the grin as she stood.

Pete gathered her in his arms and leaned forward, making her breathless with anticipation.

"I don't think that's necessary. Our police officers have been very busy since the storm. They probably wouldn't have time to arrest an amateur rule breaker like me." He pulled his head down, so close their lips grazed as he spoke. "On the other hand, I have all the time in the world."

She put her arms around Pete's neck, and her fingers brushed the lower edge of his hair.

Angela was used to always rushing, always running somewhere. It was part of being a single mom and an elected official who juggled duties at a family business as well.

But for right now, she felt time roll as slowly as ketchup making its way out of a bottle. There was no rush. Only her and Pete and the growl of the ocean a few blocks away.

She wanted to look up at the stars, wanted to see if they were beginning to twinkle and shine. She wanted to know if any of them were streaking across the sky. If she did, though, she'd have to open her eyes. And she knew when she did that, time would cease standing still. The stars would have to wait.

After all, she'd waited more than six years for a moment like this.

Pete looked at the familiar faces as members of *La Iglesia* mingled on the lawn after the Sunday morning service. The congregation was still meeting outdoors, so service times had been moved earlier in order to give everyone the best chance to beat the heat that still lingered as the calendar had segued to early October. No one rushed off after Pastor Marco finished his message, though, and it gave Pete a chance to people watch.

He noted how life's twists and turns could take you in places you never dreamed. A month ago, he didn't know any of these people, except Gloria and her family. He didn't know about the tight-knit sense of family that permeated both the *La Mission* neighborhood and the *La Iglesia* members. And now, he'd been welcomed with open arms by them, stood shoulder-to-shoulder with them at The Grace Space…and had fallen in love with one of them.

Well, make that two of them.

Angela stood a few feet away talking to two of her mother's friends who had some questions about the rebuilding of the senior citizens' center. Pete scanned and caught a glimpse of Celina, playing a game of tag with a number of other children.

Pete saw Jake Peoples tap his wife Gracie on the shoulder, then point in Pete's direction. He gave Pete a wave as he got close.

"Hey, Pete. Have you made a decision on moving forward with The Grace Space?"

Pete had lost a little sleep the last few days over the way things turned out with Mercy Medical Mission and the death of a dream he'd held for a very long time. But he'd gained the love and trust of two very special people, and he knew that ought to more than make up for it.

Angela had said she wanted him here and that tipped the scales. He wasn't going to call any more of his contacts at Mercy Medical Mission and ask for a string to be pulled or a good word to be said.

It was time to put away long-held dreams and make the most of reality.

"I think we're going to be partners, Jake. Can I come by tomorrow and sign all the paperwork?"

Jake put out his hand, and the two men shook on it. "Absolutely. I've got some things in the morning. How about late afternoon, say around four o'clock?"

"Sounds great. I'll see you then."

Jake headed back to join his little family, and Pete's heart warmed a little bit when Angela and Celina walked hand-in-hand toward him. It felt like he wasn't on the outside looking in anymore. There'd been a time when he'd dreamed of a family of his own, until cancer took it away.

Now, a hurricane had brought one to him.

Pete spent the rest of Sunday at the small pier at the end of the street with Celina, perfecting her casting skills while Angela caught up on paperwork and reading she needed to have finished before a very busy week ahead.

"Pete?" Celina asked as she held her fishing pole tightly. "I built sandcastles with my dad the other day."

"I heard about that." Pete tried to keep his voice neutral until he figured out where she was going with the conversation. He didn't want to guide the conversation or sway her thoughts on the meeting. "What did you think about it?"

"It was fun to get to go back to the beach after the hurricane. There was a lot of seaweed, though." She spoke very matter-of-factly, as if the amount of dried sargassum that had washed up on the shore was one of the bigger issues on her plate right now. Although, Pete couldn't disagree with her—it was everywhere, and as it began to dry out, the smell did permeate certain pockets of the air.

"It will be nice when everything gets cleaned up around the whole city. Your mom is working very hard to make that happen for everyone." He didn't want to influence the conversation, but he didn't want to derail it off into seaweed and beach cleanup, either, so he tried to get back on track. "So what did you think about meeting your dad?"

"He was nice. And I like the bucket that he brought me. I wonder how he knew that pink was my favorite color?"

"Probably a lucky guess. Pink is a pretty popular color. So, do you think you'd like to see him again?"

She looked down at the fishing rod in her hands. "Well, I like the idea of having a dad around, and I've never had brothers or sisters before."

The abrupt halt to Celina's train of thought signaled to Pete that the little girl had more to say. He wanted to give her a hug, to let her know that no matter what she had to say, his ears were there to listen. But since they were discussing her biological dad—and Pete wasn't even a stepdad, in fact, he wasn't even certain if Celina's mother yet thought of him as her boyfriend—he just wasn't sure what the protocol would be.

"I don't have any siblings. So, I think that part will be nice for you."

"Well yeah," Celina said with a shrug. "But Pete, if I spend more time with my dad, does that mean you and I don't get to spend as much time together? Can we still go fishing?"

Now Pete knew, without a doubt, that a hug was in order. He wrapped the little girl in his arms and gave her a squeeze.

"We will always go fishing."

9

*P*ete organized his stack of folders and prepared to wrap up the day in The Grace Space clinic a little early. He needed to be out the door in about five minutes in order to make it to the Peoples Family Foundation offices on time.

"Dr. Shipley?" A man poked his head around the curtain that divided Pete's office. Pete recognized him immediately.

"Jonas. It's good to see you." Pete put out his hand, and the two men shook hands. "What brings you by? My aunt and uncle aren't living on the island anymore. They moved to the mainland about a year ago."

Dr. Jonas Sievers had been a medical school friend of Pete's uncle Paul, and they'd remained close through the years.

He was also the medical director of the Mercy Medical Mission.

"I came looking for you, actually, Pete. I heard you called the office the other day."

Pete stuck his hands in the pocket of his lab coat. "I did. Spoke with Donna in HR."

"That's what she said. It also seems she gave you some wrong information."

Pete tried to keep a poker face on. He didn't quite know where

Jonas was going, and he didn't want to let his mind wander down any rabbit trails.

"How so?"

The older man broke into a smile. "Well, your application had already been approved. By me. And my boss, Stanley McMahon, the CEO. We have a need for someone to run our Guatemala clinic. The doctor in charge of it right now has had to leave for personal reasons and submitted a resignation straight to me. We are in a hiring freeze, but I also know how important our clinic is there. I'd gotten your application the day before I heard from Dr. Robertson. So I went down the hall to Stan's office, and we got everything worked out. I just hadn't gone to Donna yet because Dr. Robertson had a few things to take care of before making everything official. I had a meeting earlier today at Mainland Medical Center, so I decided to cross the causeway and come talk to you myself."

Pete was thankful he'd never played cards. This poker face thing was not going well. "So you're saying you've got a spot for me?"

Dr. Sievers nodded heartily. "In Guatemala. In three weeks. Are you ready to go?"

Pete noted all the signs of excitement: rapid breathing, a quickening of pulse rate. Without looking in a mirror, he couldn't be sure, but he wouldn't be surprised to see his pupils had also dilated somewhat.

"Wow, running my own clinic?" Pete knew he sounded like a kindergartener, not someone with a medical degree, but he had not seen this coming. Not only was the door to Mercy Medical Mission open again, it was *wide open*. He hadn't expected to run his own clinic—he'd fully planned on working his way up to that.

"Pete, you've run your uncle's clinic here for years. You've got ER experience and your obstetrics experience. We see a lot of births at this clinic, and I think you're the perfect candidate for the job, especially because your uncle speaks so highly of the job you've done here at the Provident Women's Health and Birth Center since he basically retired."

"I don't know what to say, Jonas. I'd spent all weekend getting over this door closing."

"Well, say you'll be on a plane to Guatemala in three weeks. That would be the perfect answer."

Pete's cell phone buzzed in his pocket. He pulled it out. On the screen flashed a text from Jake Peoples.

Running a few minutes behind, but I'm on my way—see you about 4:15.

Pete knew his pupils contracted back to normal. His breathing slowed, and his heart stopped pounding. He was supposed to be on his way to signing the paperwork with Jake.

But now that his lifelong dream was back in the picture—and better than he could have ever hoped for, Pete only had one diagnosis for his current situation: *torn-between-two-options-itis*.

"I expected to hear a yes out of you by now, Jake." The older man chuckled in the space created by Pete's silence.

Pete had known Jonas for a long time, and his uncle had known Jonas even longer. Pete knew he could shoot straight with him.

"Well, I was actually on my way to sign some paperwork." Pete explained The Grace Space and how he'd committed to Jake after talking with Donna at the end of the week.

"You said that you've got a staff of doctors and residents already in place." The senior physician spoke plainly with his words.

"That's correct, sir." Pete wasn't sure where Jonas was going with this. "With the hospital and medical school closed for likely at least the next year, things are in limbo for the medical community in Port Provident right now."

"Exactly," Jonas said, as if that explained it all. "One of them can step into your shoes here. I don't think you'll have a problem finding a doctor who can be the medical director for your grace place."

"The Grace Space. And maybe you're right. Phil Walden told me he's actually looking to take some time off from a traditional practice. He might be interested in the opportunity."

Jonas nodded. "Well, then, there's your answer. This place will continue on, and you'll get your chance to work with us at Mercy Medical Mission. I'll have Donna call you in the morning and set up a time for you to get all your paperwork done. You've got a passport, right?"

"Yes, I do. Haven't used it in a while, though."

"Now's your chance, Pete. We'll have to take care of your work and residence permits, but we should be able to get the work permit before you go—the usual turnaround is one to two months, but we've sent some nurses down there within the last two or three months, and they've been very quick to turn everything around."

"So this is really happening?" Pete felt the force of a hurricane all over again. This time it was Hurricane Jonas, moving things along with a sweeping wind of change. Pete's mind swirled, but he really didn't have time to think about any of it.

Jonas put out his hand for a handshake. "It sure is. Welcome to the Mercy Medical Mission team, Dr. Shipley. I'm excited to have you on board and to see the difference you're going to make in the world."

After Jonas passed back through the curtain, Pete took his phone out of the pocket of his white coat, then hung the coat over the back of the chair. He looked at another text from Jake and texted back that he was on his way.

But when he got there, what was he going to tell Jake?

And after that, what was he going to tell Angela?

On his way over to Jake's office, Pete called Phil Walden to see if he'd be interested in the medical director role for The Grace Space. Tori Maldonado had been doing a great job running the store and would be perfect in a full-time role managing it. Maybe this could work out after all.

Jake and Pete talked, and they conferenced Phil in on the phone to go over details. After they had a general idea of next steps, Pete got in his truck and drove east toward his home. He pulled up in the driveway and looked at the house.

It looked like this wasn't going to be his home much longer. Funny how things could change in an instant. Investors were snatching up distressed properties to rehabilitate and flip, but Pete had heard that homes like his that hadn't sustained damage and were therefore on the market at their full value were not moving at all.

He put the truck in reverse and headed back into town.

He wouldn't need to go through the hassle of selling. There were plenty of people who needed a permanent home to call their own in Port Provident right now. Especially one with a pier at the end of the street that was perfect for fishing.

Pete knew exactly what he would do with his house. He hoped that would make things easier for Angela and Celina. Telling them would be the hardest thing he'd have to do between now and when his plane left for Central America.

As he drove, Angela filled his thoughts. He knew he had fallen in love with her, her sparkling sugar eyes and her generous and determined spirit. But he didn't really know where they stood. She'd said she wanted him to stay in Port Provident and run The Grace Space, but that could have been as much for what the facility could do for the community as it was for him. He'd kissed her and thought about kissing her even more than that—and he knew she'd kissed him back—but was that enough to give up the dream he'd had for years?

Angela was a practical sort, and Pete could already hear her laughing at the fact that he'd even mulled the question over in her mind. No woman who was leading a city through the tangled business of hurricane recovery would let sentimentality keep her from her goals and the dreams she had for making Port Provident a better place.

She'd tell him it was the same for him. He'd had a dream and he'd fully pursued it until three days ago—when there'd apparently been a misunderstanding.

Pete pulled through the gate at the RV park and angled his truck in front of Angela's temporary residence. He got out and headed for the door, grateful for the time he'd had to think on the way here from his house.

He didn't even need to ask Angela what she thought. He knew what she'd say. Stay the course. Follow your dreams.

He would. Even though he knew that would lead him away from Angela and Celina.

Pete knocked on the door and tried to put a smile on his face. This course of action was the right one, and letting them live in his house for as long as they needed to was a good thing. Celina deserved a real house with her own room and a fishing pier that she could see from her bedroom window.

He was making the practical decision. The right decision.

Angela opened the door and her face curved into a smile as she saw Pete. "I was just making dinner. Celina's playing with a friend down the street, but she'll be back in about fifteen minutes to eat. Why don't you come on in and you can tell me how everything went with Jake today."

There would be no easing into the subject. Pete decided he would just think of it as giving a difficult diagnosis to the patient. He'd done that plenty of times before. Stay compassionate but focused on the facts. That was the practical approach, and again, he'd already reminded himself that Angela valued practicality.

"Well, as good as dinner sounds, that's actually what I came to talk to you about. There's been a development."

Angela moved place settings on the table and brought a third plate from the cabinet. "A development? That sounds interesting. Jake was in a meeting with me right before he headed back to do the paperwork with you. He didn't tell me anything had changed."

Stay practical. Don't beat around the bush, Pete.

Pete didn't pray much, but he took a deep breath and asked God to send him the right words, the practical words.

"As I was heading out the door for my meeting, my uncle's good friend, Dr. Jonas Sievers, stopped by The Grace Space to talk with me."

"Does he work at Provident Medical Center?"

Pete took a few steps to the couch and sat down. "No, he's the medical director for Mercy Medical Mission."

"Oh," Angela said, a puzzled tone in her voice.

"He said there had been a miscommunication when I talked to the lady in HR last week. They have a spot for me, running a clinic in Guatemala, starting in three weeks. He said I'm the perfect candidate for the job—and it's pretty exciting that they want to put me in charge of one of their larger clinics to begin with."

Angela opened a drawer and pulled out silverware. "I bet that was hard for you to tell them you'd already committed to The Grace Space and Jake's offer."

Pete felt some of the same reactions he had earlier when Jonas first dropped the Guatemala news on him. "Well, I didn't actually tell him no."

She dropped the fork on the table with a crash. "Why not? You have a job running a clinic now. Here. In Port Provident."

"I've always been up front that working with Mercy Medical Mission has been my dream for years. I've connected Jake with Dr. Phil Walden, a friend of mine and professor at the medical school. I think he's going to step in and run the clinic side of The Grace Space. He was very interested. So don't worry about Port Provident, Madam Mayor—The Grace Space will still be around to serve the community."

"And you're just going to go. After our whole conversation Friday night about there being a foundation to build on?" She didn't look up, but instead straightened dishes that weren't even crooked.

"I have to, Angela. This is my chance to go. They're in a hiring freeze. I won't get another opportunity like this for a long time."

He was doing what he planned to do—keep it practical. But seeing her face change from a warm glow to cold stone was practically his undoing.

Angela picked up a plate, fork, and glass and took two steps back into the small kitchen and began opening drawers and cabinets, putting the items away. "Then I think you need to go. Celina will be home soon, and I don't want you to be around."

Pete's heart unraveled. "You don't want me around Celina?"

"No. Not if you're going to leave and never come back. She's spent her whole life without a father. He's back in her life now, but I'm still not sure exactly what that will wind up being. I'm not going to have another man that she looks up to—the man who has become the real father figure in her life—leave after she gets more and more attached to him. It's best that you just go now. I'll find some way to explain it to her."

Pete opened his mouth, then quickly closed it. He'd already pegged Angela as practical. She'd certainly lived up to it right now—brutally practical.

He walked out the door and down the two small metal steps.

The door to the truck closed with a loud thud that reverberated in his ears and his soul. Pete felt like he was losing Anna all over again—someone he loved was being taken out of his life, and he didn't have control over it.

At least he'd gotten to tell Anna goodbye.

Two weeks later, Angela was unpacking the last box of her things in the mayor's office. She'd finally gotten all of her furniture and books and other décor transferred from her City Council office at the end of the hall. She placed a framed photo of her and Celina on the beach at the corner of her desk. She'd always loved this photo of giving her daughter a bear hug because it reminded her of the bond they shared.

Last week, Celina had asked questions periodically about Pete. Angela tried to keep her answers light and even promised she'd learn how to fish so Celina wouldn't have to give up her new favorite hobby. But this week, Celina hadn't mentioned him once.

Maybe she had moved past it already, demonstrating that resilience kids were known for.

Angela wished she could have said the same. Pete popped into her thoughts more often than she cared to admit and lingered there for longer than she was comfortable. He'd be on a plane to Central America soon, and maybe when she knew he was gone for good, she could banish the thoughts of him for good.

She still had her daughter, her family, her church, and the good people of Port Provident—and that was what mattered most to her. Not the presence of one doctor on an island full of them. Not even one who was a good kisser and made her believe in wishes made on shooting stars.

A knock sounded at the door to her office. Angela raised her voice loud enough to be heard and asked them to let themselves in.

"This was just dropped off for you." Carter Porter, a city councilman, held out an envelope.

Angela walked out from behind her desk and took the folded white square of paper. "Thanks, Carter. Who's it from?"

Mail service was still spotty on the island, and this didn't have a stamp on it, so clearly it had been hand-delivered.

"Not sure. It was a teenager. I don't think it was actually from him. I doubt you're being invited to a rave or anything."

"A rave?" Angela laughed out loud, the first time she remembered doing so since Pete had walked out the door of her trailer. "Carter, I don't think people have raves anymore. And even if they do, I seriously doubt anyone is inviting me to one. You've known me for how long?"

"Well, it was pre-hurricane. Everything else is kind of a blur."

"Four years, Carter. We've been on City Council together for four years. But I hear you on the pre-hurricane and post-hurricane thing. Time feels very different right now."

Carter nodded in agreement. "It does indeed, but we'll soon be back to the way things used to be."

The way things used to be...in some ways, Angela knew she was already there. Pete was already out of her life. The way things used to be.

Carter whistled a pop tune as he walked down the hallway toward his office. Angela opened the envelope and scanned the piece of paper folded inside. It was an invitation to the grand opening of the new, permanent location for The Grace Space at the end of the week.

Her first instinct told her to say no. Then, she looked at the calendar on the wall. Pete would be on his way to Guatemala by then. He wouldn't be there.

As the mayor, she needed to be there to support this home-grown program that was making a difference in the lives of hundreds of people in Port Provident. And as a woman, she needed to make peace with not thinking of Pete every time she went somewhere that brought up a memory.

There was no better place to start that than The Grace Space this Friday. She picked up the phone and called the number to RSVP yes.

At the end of the week, Angela held Celina's hand as they walked in the door of the new location of The Grace Space. Someone had taken one of the emergency roof tarps and created a giant blue bow to hang out front. It made Angela smile a little bit to see a little whimsy coming out of something that was so ubiquitous and utilitarian all across the town.

Celina patted the puff of the bow as they passed. Angela decided to bring her daughter to the opening, even though she herself was here in an official capacity. She wanted Celina to see how a community could come together for good. As mayor, Angela was grateful for all the help Port Provident had received. But seeing the citizens of Port Provident work together in a grassroots way made her the most proud.

"Mama! Look!" Celina tugged on Angela's hand as soon as they walked through the front door. "It's Pete! He's here!"

Angela felt her stomach plummet down to her toes. He was supposed to be gone. He had chosen Guatemala. Why was he here?

Celina let go of her mother's hand and took off toward Pete down one of the aisles of merchandise in this lower floor of The Grace Space that clearly served as the store part of the operation. Angela hesitated. Her heart wouldn't let her follow. But her mind reminded her that she looked ridiculous standing in the doorway.

She looked around for someone to talk to, but everyone nearby already seemed engaged in their own conversations.

Didn't anyone want to talk to the mayor?

Wasn't there a baby she could kiss somewhere in this place?

Something…anything to shake the feeling that Dr. Pete Shipley was looking in her direction.

"Angela." She'd been trying to shake the memory of that voice out of her head for two weeks. Now she knew it was never going to happen, no matter how far away he went or how long he was gone.

"I thought you had a plane to catch."

"I did," he said.

A staffer from the Peoples Family Foundation tapped him on the shoulder before he could say anything more. "Dr. Shipley? It's time to start the ceremony. Jake is going to introduce you so that you can speak."

Good. Angela scanned the room, resuming her search for a baby to plant a smooch on. She didn't have a role to play in this, so she could stand as far away from Pete as possible and still be inside the building and do the mayor support thing. That suited her just fine.

What no longer suited her just fine was bringing Celina. Today should have been a great teachable moment to show her what a special community she lived in. Instead, now Angela was going to be facing more days, and possibly weeks, of questions about Pete from a little girl who had to learn the hard way that people could make a place in your heart and then just leave without a trace.

Jake said a few words and then handed the microphone over to Pete. Angela didn't hear any of them. All she heard were the running arguments in her head about why was Pete Shipley still here and what was she going to do about it?

Angela tried to look out the window. It was blocked by a display, but that was better than looking straight ahead at Pete. Because every time she did that, she noticed how just a little bit of chest hair showed at the point of the v-neck of his light blue scrubs. And she certainly didn't need to notice how the light from the front windows played on the highlights of his hair where it was streaked with those early streaks of silver that she'd once thought made him look distinguished and thoughtful. And downright attractive.

Most importantly of all, not looking at his face as he spoke kept her from remembering the times when both their faces had been a feather's width apart as they stood under the glitter of the stars off the Texas coast.

Too bad that turning her head didn't turn off her ears, though.

"I came to be a part of The Grace Space almost by accident. I had some extra time on my hands after my own medical practice was wiped out by the storm, and Pastor Marco Ruiz at *La Iglesia de la Luz del Mundo* needed some help organizing a few trucks of donations that had flooded in. While I was there, I met some members of *La Iglesia* who had a pressing need for some basic medical care that we were lacking on the island with the close of our major medical facilities. After some brainstorming, the idea for The Grace Space came together, and I'm proud to say this is a homegrown initiative."

The crowd clapped, and Angela found herself clapping along with them. She also found herself looking straight ahead, straight at Pete.

He caught her eye and pointed, then waved for her to join him. She hesitated, but the crowd parted a bit to allow her clearance, and she knew she couldn't just stay put at her spot in the back of the room.

"I'd like to invite the acting mayor of Port Provident, Angela Ruiz, to join me up here. Most of you in this room probably know Angela. She doesn't just care about Port Provident. She loves Port Provident. And if there's one thing I've learned in my time as a resident of Port Provident—especially since Hurricane Hope came to town—it's that you can never have too many people who love you. Right, Angela?"

Angela felt a reflexive smile pop across her face. She couldn't let the citizens in front of her know how his words caught her off-guard. They couldn't know the memories his words stirred in her heart.

She'd thought she was falling in love with this man. And then...he just planned to leave after telling her he wanted to stay. She just didn't know. All she knew is she had to just stand here and smile, support The Grace Space and the people in her community who came through here.

The rest, she'd figure out later—after Pete got on a plane to Guatemala and she wouldn't be caught off-guard like this ever again where this particular doctor was concerned.

Pete began to speak again. "For a long time, I've been interested in serving in a medical mission overseas. A few weeks ago, I was offered the opportunity to direct a clinic in Guatemala. But during the past two weeks, as I started to put together transition plans for another colleague of mine to take over the running of The Grace Space, I realized I didn't want to just go serve in any community. I wanted to serve *this* community. Port Provident has become a second family to me. And I'm looking forward to staying here, putting down roots, and growing the good that can be done through The Grace Space."

The crowd began to clap again. The enthusiasm across the room rang in Angela's ears.

And so did Pete's words.

He wasn't going to Guatemala. He was staying in Port Provident to serve the people in Port Provident.

The smile dropped from Angela's face because she needed to bite her lip in order to keep her emotions in check. Pete wrapped up his remarks and then took Angela's hand.

It was the middle of the afternoon. There were no shooting stars around. But there was no denying the crackle of electricity that shot across her palm and back up through her wrist as Pete's hand cupped around hers. It was as potent as the energy generated by a million solar systems out in the sky.

"Can I talk to you for a moment?" His voice lowered and hovered somewhere just above a whisper. "Come over here. We can talk over here on the housewares aisle."

Pete guided her to the end of the aisle, dishes on one side and drinking glasses on the other. It felt completely ordinary and domestic. Angela wished she could say the same, but nothing about her emotions or her racing heart felt ordinary.

"I'm not going to Guatemala."

"I heard that." She hoped he couldn't hear the quiver in her voice. Maybe if she didn't say much, he wouldn't notice.

"I meant what I said up there. Port Provident has become like a second family to me. I realized I belong here." He held her hand a little tighter. "But another thing I realized while I was thinking everything over was that I don't want a second family. I want a first family. I want to grill dinner on the deck with you and unwind at the end of a day. I want to take Celina fishing. I want to put down roots in Port Provident so I can watch Celina grow, and I can see how your vision to rebuild this city comes to play out. I don't just want to be a part of Port Provident, Angela. I want to be a part of your life, Celina's life. *Our life*. I want to serve in this community because it's your community—because it's *our* community, our daughter's community. I've had a dream to do medical mission work for a long time, but God has shown me that I don't need to go halfway around the world to make a difference. It came down to what your nephew Marco told me early on—that verse from Jeremiah—if you seek the welfare of the city where you are, you'll find your own welfare there too."

As Angela tried to sort through the tumble and roll of her feelings, Celina came running up and crashed into her with a hug.

"Mama! Pete's staying here! Isn't it great?" Her little girl's eyes twinkled just like the stars which had occupied so many of her thoughts lately.

In the end, it all came back to the stars.

They couldn't shine enough on their own, but together, they were powerful. She looked over Pete's shoulder at the store and clinic he'd brought to life, then thought of the ideas she wanted to bring to life for Port Provident. And then she looked down at her daughter, the gift she loved more than life itself.

She couldn't do everything she wanted to do for her daughter or her city alone. But together? The sky was the limit.

"It is great, Sweetie. You can never have too many people to love."

EPILOGUE

*A*ngela Ruiz looked around the gymnasium of Provident High School. Rows and rows of tables had been set with turkeys and dressing and sweet potatoes and gravy and salad and cranberries. The doors were about to open for the first-ever Port Provident Thanksgiving Feast, a community-wide celebration of thanks for all the progress the residents of Port Provident had made in rebuilding the city they called home.

This had all been Pete's idea, and he'd worked with contacts from all across the state that he'd met through The Grace Space. Everything here had been donated by churches and generous people from across Texas who wanted to help the citizens of Port Provident have a holiday truly worth celebrating.

Jennifer Parker from the *Port Provident Herald* strode purposefully across the gym. Angela took a deep breath, hoping for some softball questions today. After all, it was Thanksgiving. And this was a celebration. Hopefully, Jennifer would go easy on her.

"Hi, Jennifer." Angela greeted her City Hall beat reporter as Jennifer's photographer walked behind her, setting up for a photo. Angela noticed Pete and Celina putting the finishing touches on a basket full of rolls at the table closest to her. The *click-click-click* of the camera echoed in the large room.

"Hi, Mayor Ruiz. Happy Thanksgiving."

Angela smoothed the front of her brown sweater. "I think they're getting ready to open the doors, so we should probably make this quick —I try not to stand between people and a room full of turkeys."

Jennifer chuckled a bit. "Actually, I've got most everything I need for this story. But I was talking with Dr. Shipley earlier and it turns out there is a pretty pressing question that needs to be asked about the future of Port Provident."

So much for the holiday softball line of questioning. Jennifer Parker never took a day off.

"That's fine, Jennifer. You know I'll always answer if I'm able."

Pete and Celina finished their photo op with the rolls and walked over just to the side of Angela and the reporter.

"Dr. Shipley, did you want to ask?"

Angela looked at Pete, then over at Jennifer, then back at Pete again. "Since when did you get a press pass?"

She tried to laugh at her own joke, but Angela couldn't brush off the butterflies in her stomach. She'd been asked hundreds of questions by Jennifer Parker over the years. Something wasn't adding up here.

"Jennifer's letting me borrow hers, just this once."

"You can't borrow media credentials, Pete. That's not how it works."

He smiled, then took a step closer and reached for her hand. Before she registered what was happening, Pete dropped to one knee on the gray-and-white flecked vinyl tile.

"Well, if you want to tell your Public Information Officer on me, I guess you can. But I think you might want to listen to what I have to say."

The butterflies in her stomach began to circle madly.

"Angela, today's a day when we are supposed to give thanks for the blessings in our lives, and the biggest one in my life this year has been Hurricane Hope. I know it sounds crazy, but because of the storm, I had the chance to open The Grace Space and I met you. Not long after the hurricane, a very wise little girl said that you can never have too many people who love you. She was right. And I love you and her. There are plenty of people who love you both, but I love you both more, and I want to spend the rest of my life with you."

He pulled out a box from his pocket and flipped it open to reveal three diamonds together on a platinum band.

"One for you. One for Celina. One for me. I picked this one to represent the family I never expected I'd be so blessed to have. Angela Ruiz, will you marry me?"

Pete plucked the ring out of the velvet box and held it right at the tip of her ring finger, waiting. Angela hadn't seen anything shine that brightly since the night of the meteor shower on his deck.

"Yes. Absolutely yes." She held out her hand, separating her fingers just enough for Pete to slide the ring on. "You can never have too much love."

You Don't Have to Leave Port Provident!
Start His Texas Princess Now

Recovery works best when everyone lends a helping hand. When a princess from Port Provident's sister city comes to Texas, big dreams have a chance to be fulfilled. Your presence is cordially requested by Her Royal Highness Princess Anneliese of San Petro as the Port Provident: Hurricane Hope series continues.

HIS TEXAS PRINCESS

**HE CAME TO REPAIR DAMAGED HOUSES. SHE CAME TO
REPAIR HER DAMAGED HEART...**

Her Royal Highness Princess Anneliese de Cotriaro is trying to find
her place in the world--and in the kingdom of San Petro, a small
paradise off the coast of Central America. She believes there is more to
her life than simply being "the spare" to the crown's heir and having
her every move followed by paparazzi after a broken engagement.
Because Port Provident, Texas, is a sister city to San Petro's capital city
of Rosada, when Princess Anneliese sees the images of destruction
from Hurricane Hope in the news, she knows this is the opportunity
she's been praying for to show she's a woman of substance.

Matt McGregor is used to disasters. Working with Helping Hands
Homes, he's returned to his hometown after the hurricane with an
ambitious goal to renovate 100 damaged homes by Christmas. When
the national office tells him they've been able to score a PR opportunity
with the visiting princess of San Petro to work on one of the houses
and help raise the funds they'll need to achieve their goals, Matt sees
imminent disaster. Building a house is hard work and he needs

committed volunteers--not a prissy princess who is sure to be afraid to get her hands dirty.

Can a princess in search of a mission make a difference in the world of a blue-collar man who can't afford distractions to his work?

Read the Complete Port Provident: Hurricane Hope Series

WANT MORE OF PORT PROVIDENT?

Would you like a reader-exclusive free Port Provident story?
Join my reader society today and get A Place to Find Love, a sweet
escape Port Provident romance, available only for newsletter
subscribers!
https://www.subscribepage.com/kristenethridgenewsletter

CAN I ASK YOU FOR A SMALL FAVOR?

If you liked this story, I'd like to ask you to please leave a review. Help me spread the word about Port Provident on Amazon. Most major retailers depend on an algorithm to boost a book's visibility among readers browsing for new titles. Reviews play a major role in how those algorithms work.

I'd appreciate your help in letting other readers just like you know about *Shelter from the Storm*'s hope, heart, and happily-ever-after. It's not about the length of the review—even just a few words like "Good story—I enjoyed it" may seem simple, but can help other readers like you know this is a story worth picking up.

PORT PROVIDENT: HURRICANE HOPE SERIES

Read the Entire Port Provident: Hurricane Hope Series

Shelter from the Storm
The Doctor's Unexpected Family
His Texas Princess
Holiday of Hope

Love Hallmark movies? Pick up Kristen's book October Kiss, based on the Hallmark movie viewers love! Available anywhere books are sold —in paperback, digital, and audio!
October Kiss from Hallmark Publishing

ABOUT KRISTEN

Kristen Ethridge writes Sweet Escape Romance—stories with hope, heart and happily-ever-after—for Harlequin's Love Inspired line, Hallmark Publishing, and Laurel Lock Publishing. She's a Romance Writers of America Golden Heart Award nominee and both an Amazon Christian Fiction and Inspirational Romance #1 Best-Selling Author.

You can find Kristen in her native habitat—a Texas patio—where she's likely to be savoring the joy of a crispy taco, along with a glass of iced tea. Scents from her essential oil diffuser are also a must, since she's a certified aromatherapist. She's almost convinced her family that it's normal to talk to imaginary people, as long it goes in a book.

Find her online at http://www.kristenethridge.com and on Amazon and Bookbub. You can get a free story for signing up for her newsletter at https://www.subscribepage.com/kristenethridgenewsletter. You can also follow her adventures in writing at www. facebook.com/kristenethridgebooks.

www.kristenethridge.com
https://www.facebook.com/KristenEthridgeBooks
https://instagram.com/kristenethridge

Don't forget...if you love sweet escape romances, join Kristen's newsletter!

ACKNOWLEDGMENTS

The Grace Space is modeled on a real community event, organized by First Baptist Church of Galveston, Texas, in the wake of Hurricane Ike. The medical clinic was staffed with students, residents and doctors from the University of Texas Medical Branch and members of the church lovingly laid donations out on water-damaged pews so that members of the Galveston community could come take what they needed to begin rebuilding their lives.

To the members of First Baptist Church of Galveston who served the Galveston community with a tireless heart and the churches like Park Cities Baptist of Dallas, Texas, who stood behind Galveston and sent people to be the hands and hearts of Jesus on the ground for months after the storm, this book is for you. Thank you for your compassion and generosity.

∼

"Each of you should use whatever gift you have received to serve others, as faithful stewards of God's grace in its various forms."
—1 PETER 4:10

~

Made in the USA
Monee, IL
03 February 2021